Enraged

Dedication

To the ones that sat down at tables they should have fucking flipped.

Jolene

"Happy Wedding Day, Bitchhhh!"

Opening one eye, I confirmed what I already knew. The friendly, loud voice belonged to my childhood best friend Cassie.

"Good morning, Cass." I rolled over to face her.

"Why, Miss Jolene Grace Felder, are you still in bed? You are getting married today!" Her eyes glittered with excitement.

"I know!" I sat up and stretched. "I had a hard time falling asleep last night."

She frowned at me.

"It's just those pesky, pre-wedding jitters, Lena. Just remember, the next time you wake up, you'll be Mrs. Jace Reynolds!"

Realizing she was right, I grinned.

You've wanted to marry this man since sophomore year, Lena. Tell your anxiety to fuck off.

Before she could continue her Maid of Honor peptalk, her iPhone rang.

"Sorry, babe, it's Dak," she explained before leaving the room.

Climbing out of bed, I stretched and stumbled to the bathroom to wash my face. Even though I've lived here with Jace for over a year now, our master bathroom still smells like I don't exist. Switching on the warm water, I inhaled, taking in every bit of the scent of leather, mouthwash, expensive cologne, and the faintest hint of smoke.

Even the Glade plug ins and my Scentsy warmers I added don't hold a candle to all things Jace.

"Lena?"

"In here!" I called out.

Cassie appeared in the bathroom doorway.

"Dak said Jace is so nervous!" She giggled. "I reminded him he better be taking notes because he will be the groom in a few short months!"

They had the right idea planning a spring wedding. Why the hell did I decide to do this in December?

"I'm nervous, too," I admitted. "Blaine will be here in an hour to do our hair. Mama, Bailey, and Bristol will be here anytime now."

My best friend nodded.

You're reminding her of shit she already knows, Lena.

Cassie walked over to Jace's side of the vanity. Grabbing the Crest Brilliance, I started brushing my teeth. She watched me in the mirror, grabbing bottles of my fiancé's cologne to smell while she waited for me to finish.

"You sure about this Lena?" She sat a bottle of Dior's Sauvage back on the vanity.

Sure about what?

"About getting married?"

She nodded.

"Yes," I assured her. "Why do you ask?"

Hopping on the counter, she stared at me.

"I'm just checking. I know it can be kinda scary, knowing you won't ever be with anyone else."

"I guess that's another perk of all of us being high school sweethearts," I joked. "Neither of us will ever experience those first-time jitters ever again."

She gave me a small smile.

"Do you feel like you've missed out on anything these last fifteen years by only being with Jace?" She questioned.

Fifteen years makes it sound like it's been forever.

"No," I concluded. "You and Dakota got together a few weeks after Jace and I started dating. Do you ever regret being a one and done?"

"I'm satisfied completely. I wouldn't change a thing." She promised.

It has been a wonderful fifteen years.

Springing off the countertop, she wrapped me in a hug.

"Come on, Mrs. Reynolds, let's get you some breakfast before we get you married."

Twenty minutes later, I had forced myself to choke down a cinnamon raisin bagel and a cup of coffee. I silently willed nerves to settle so I could keep it down.

"Lee Leeeee!" My mama's voice rang out. "It's your wedding day!"

She walked in the front door without knocking, something she never does. She skipped into the kitchen, my sister-in-law Bailey and niece Bristol right behind her.

"Aunt Lee Lee, Mama said I get to wear my princess dress today!"

I grinned.

My sweet niece was my favorite person in the entire world.

My older brother, Cruise, had met Bailey when she first moved to Creek's Edge. She was an Army widow, barely surviving her grief and her adaptation to a new town when she and Cruise stumbled across one another at Deja Brew, our local coffee shop. Three years later, they were married, and Bailey was pregnant with a little girl that would be named Bristol Jolene Felder. Bailey still struggled with the grief of losing her first husband, but my brother made sure to remind her often that his memory would never be forgotten. Bristol's first name was chosen after the name of the racetrack, Bristol Motor Speedway, where Bailey met her fallen soldier all those years ago. Now, at four years old, our sweet little toddler tornado lived up to her name – always 90mph or nothing, loud and full of energy.

"Aunt Lee Lee gets to dress up like a princess today, Bristy Boo!" My sister-in-love reminded her.

On cue, my mama's eyes filled with tears, but my Maid of Honor and my Matron of Honor were one step ahead of me with crying control.

"Alexa, play Y2K hits!" Cassie hollered at the smart device.

Always obedient, Alexa began blaring Usher.

My mama, always the emotional one, pulled me to the side.

"Did you eat?" She questioned.

"Yes, ma'am, I ate a little. I'm so nervous!"

"No need to be nervous, Sugar. This day has been a long time coming!" She pulled me into her embrace. "You haven't seen Jace since the rehearsal, right? It's bad luck!"

"No ma'am, I haven't." I promised, hoping she wouldn't see right through my lying eyes.

Truth is, last night, Jace and I had met around midnight at our old secret hiding spot for one last quickie before we were legally bound.

That man and his hips will always be lethal on a tailgate in the back of a dark field.

The doorball rang.

"I'll get it! Gotta be Blaine!" Cassie jumped up.

Rushing to my bedroom, I peeled off my ratty Creek's Edge High School t-shirt and pajama shorts, replacing it with my monogrammed bridal robe. I tied it tightly around my waist before heading back into the den to join the others.

Fuck, I want to shower. I hate showering the night before an event.

"There is my gorgeous bride!" Blaine beamed at me. "How are we doing this morning, beautiful?"

"Like I wish I could have showered!" I half joked. "How are you?"

He gave me a confused look.

"Why can't you shower?"

Ummm… because you told me not to.

"You said not to, right?" I reminded him. "I showered last night but I still just feel gross."

He laughed a hearty laugh. "Sis, I told you not to shower and wash your hair because I need it a tad oily for your updo, but in no way was I telling you not to wash your ass."

He covered his mouth as he remembered Bristol was in the room, but Bailey was laughing.

"Oh." I felt silly.

"I'll do Mama and the girls first. Go clean your clam, love bug!"

Nodding, I took off for my bathroom.

"No hair wetting!" He called after me.

"Got it!"

I turned the shower knob to the warmest setting and slipped out of my robe while I waited for it to heat up. Admiring my bronze skin, I mentally thanked the girl at our local spray tan boutique.

I look like I've been tanning in Maui instead of freezing half to death in Georgia.

As I stepped into the shower, I winced as the scalding water cascaded over my skin. As I lathered my body, my nervousness returned.

I'm so ready to get past the scary part and get to the cabin.

I don't know how long I stood there scrubbing my thighs, but it was long enough for Blaine to tap on the glass shower door.

Startled, I shrieked.

"Relax, honey," he quieted me. "You don't have anything that I didn't see and rule out in high school."

I laughed.

Blaine was new to Creek's Edge, having moved here less than a year ago after he lost his husband of five years. He came into the bank to speak with us about a home loan and I fell in love with him instantly. His energy and light, despite the loss he had endured, was such a privilege to be witness.

The idea of falling in love is scary as it is, but the idea that you may have to live without your person is fuckin' terrifying.

I shuddered at the idea of losing Jace.

"Everyone is done but little miss princess. I couldn't remember if you wanted her hair a certain way, if she or Bailey had certain ideas or if I have creative freedom," he explained his interruption.

"Whatever they want is fine. If they don't have any specific ideas, you have complete creative freedom."

"Perfect!" He beamed. "Her curls are a dream to work with!"

"Her mama would probably disagree with you. She says she looks like Beetlejuice when she first wakes up."

His laugh echoed off my bathroom tile as he pointed to the invisible watch on his wrist.

"Get out the damn shower. You're getting married in two hours!" He faked exasperation, rolling his eyes.

"Be out in two minutes," I promised.

Two minutes and forty-six steps later, I was sitting across from Bristol as he swept her beautiful curls into a less extravagant version of the hairdo that he and I had planned for myself. Bristol smiled at me; a sweet mischievous smile that made me wonder how the gears inside her little mind were turning. I thought back to the Flower Girl Discussion from eight months ago.

Of course, she can be your flower girl, but the problem is, she may not act right," Cruise explained. "Sometimes, she just wakes up and decides to be a terrorist."

"She will be the perfect flower girl because she is unapologetically herself," I responded. "If she decides she wants to toss petals, she can, if she decides she wants to yeet the basket at the guests, that's okay, too."

"Dear Lord, let's not encourage her madness," Bailey insisted. "Let's pray she will wake up and be the sweet little girl we are trying to raise her to be!"

Truth is, I was looking forward to watching her walk down the aisle because I was curious to see what she would do.

We all watched in companionable silence as he twisted and pinned Bristol's curly hair. He finished in record time, sending my sweet niece to my bedroom to approve his work.

"Now the beautiful bride!" Blaine tapped the seat of my dining room chair. I sat down obediently, doing my best to stifle a moan as he combed my scalp with his fingers.

Head messages and hair tickles are second to none.

Alexa continued with her Y2K playlist. As Blaine twisted his expensive golden curling iron through my long blonde hair, Nelly serenaded us.

"The higher the hair, the closer to heaven!" He reminded me as he teased and pinned. From the corner of the chaise lounge, Bailey snorted, clearly amused by the fact that he had quoted Dolly Parton.

Being named Jolene, I had heard Dolly jokes all my life.

Thanks, Mama.

About a hundred and sixty bobby pins and half a can of hairspray later, my hair was swept into the curly, messy luxurious updo that I had picked out from Pinterest.

Blaine passed me a handheld mirror and I gasped. He had far exceeded my expectations, turning my long locks into something you'd see in a movie.

I have bridal hair.

From beside me, he beamed, obviously thrilled that I loved the way he had transformed a bank loan officer slash candle company owner into a bridal beauty.

"Now, we do makeup!" He clapped his hands.

"I think since you're about to get makeup and then Mama will help you get dressed, I'm going to head on over to the church and make sure everything is perfect and ready to go," Cassie spoke up.

"That would be awesome, honey. The wedding coordinator is there but we both know how subpar she has been, so I'd appreciate you making sure everything is the way that Lena and Jace want it!" My mama encouraged me.

Cassie sprang to her feet. "I'll take my dress with me and throw it on after I've triple checked everything!" She promised.

She patted my shoulder as she made her way to the front door.

Hopefully, everything is as it should be and she's able to just go chill in the bride's room.

"Aunt Lee Lee, are you gonna wear lipstick?"

Bristol's sweet voice brought me back to the present.

"Yes ma'am, I am!"

Kneeling in front of me, Blaine gave me a hundred-watt smile.

It was in that moment that I made the executive decision to tell my nerves to fuck off. I sat back and enjoyed getting to be the princess for the day.

A blink of an eye later, we pulled up to Creek's Edge Baptist Church.

My mama, always the one to be counted on, was out of the driver's side of her car and around to the back seat to help me and my gigantic dress out into the world.

"Lift it so it doesn't drag!" She instructed. "We can't have a bruised looking bustle!"

What the fuck is a bruised lookin' bustle, Mama?

I lifted my dress the way she demanded, making damn sure not an inch of it touched the ground. My mama's sister, Evelyn, stood at the side entrance to the church.

"Hurry up, sugar! The coast is clear, but we need to get you to the bride's room!"

The coast will remain clear until the ceremony, Aunt Evie. Jace is probably doing Jack Daniels shots with all the guys from the department and talking about structure fires.

Nonetheless, I hustled my way into the back hallway of the fellowship hall, where three more aunts, a cousin, and my Mamaw waited for me.

After a round of oohs and ahhs, I excused myself to take a breather in the bathroom. Within thirty seconds, there was a knock at the door.

"Lena?"

Mama.

"Yes, ma'am, I'm coming. I just needed a second to breathe and steady my nerves."

Opening the door, I swished and swayed to get myself and my gown through the doorway without injury to either of us.

"We are starting in twenty minutes and can't seem to find Cassie, but I have to go find your daddy and make sure his bowtie is straight," she complained.

I couldn't help but smile, already knowing my daddy's bowtie was, without a doubt, more crooked than a politician.

"I'll find her. She's probably in her mama's office."

Cassie's mama had been the church secretary since we were little so if there was anywhere in the building she would be, it was probably her office.

"Ok, go find her, I'll go check on Daddy, and we will be back. Wanna bet on how long it takes him once he sees you to start crying?" She joked.

"The second he lays eyes on me!"

It was no secret that I was a daddy's girl.

I was the apple of his eye, and everyone knew it. From the time I could walk, I was outside with him, helping feed the animals and riding on the tractor.

Married or not, my ass is still gonna be a daddy's girl.

I set off down the hallway to Mrs. Mellie's office. As I rounded the last corner, I heard Cassie's voice.

Told ya, Mama.

But her voice wasn't the only voice I heard. There was a second voice; a man's voice.

Jace?

Pushing open the office door, I felt my soul leave my body.

Standing before me with her satin, lavender gown hiked around her hips and her elbows braced on her mama's desk, was my best friend since kindergarten. And behind her?

Behind her was the love of my life with his tuxedo pants around his ankles.

The world froze around me. Time stopped, as did the two people I loved most.

"Lena!" My best friend called out.

But I was beyond words.

"Lena, did you find –," my mama's voice stopped dead in its tracks. "Oh my God."

I should have jumped across that desk and beat somebody's ass.

I should have reminded my mama not to take the Lord's name in vain, especially while in church.

I should have cussed both Cassie and Jace for all they were worth – which really wasn't much at all.

I should have done…something.

Instead, I turned and ran, my four-foot dress train dragging behind me.

I ran and ran until I got to the parking lot. Glancing around, I mentally thanked my piece of shit fiancé for driving my car to the church… and for leaving the keys inside.

Wordlessly, I stuffed myself into the driver side of my SUV and pulled from the parking lot, leaving behind everything and everyone I knew and loved, including the person I was just five minutes before.

You said we couldn't have a bruised bustle, Mama… what about a bruised Bride?

Dakota

"I'm not sure of the science behind it, but it's absolute facts that women love a man in a tuxedo," Carter explained.

I rolled my eyes.

"You say the same thing about us when we are in our turnouts," I reminded him.

"I'm not wrong about that, neither. Hey Dane, tell Dak about that time –"

"Don't tell me about any time," I interrupted. "I don't want to hear about any of y'all's shenanigans over on B- shift."

Before he could protest, shouting rang out from down the church corridor.

"On your WEDDING DAY no less!" A familiar voice hollered. "Her best friend!"

Carter, Dane, and I exchanged looks.

"Hell, I'll go see what's happening," I announced.

I feel like this falls under the best man duties; putting out any fires that may arise on Jace and Jolene's wedding day.

Stepping out into the hallway, I glanced around. Near the entrance to the sanctuary, I found the source of the shouting.

Is that Lena's daddy? What in the world?

As I quickly made my way down the hallway, the situation seemed to escalate.

"I'll knock the fuck out of you and see if you regain some clarity!" Brett Felder shouted.

Sir, this is a church house.

"Hey y'all, what in the world is goin' on?" I questioned, trying my best to diffuse the situation.

Lena's daddy turned towards me, eyes flashing.

"Ask your girlfriend!" He spat out.

Fiancée.

It was only then that I noticed Cassie standing between Mr. Felder and Jace. Her cheeks were streaked with mascara and her neat hair had come undone. As I took in the sight of her, the words I had overheard before coming down the hall flooded my mind.

On your wedding day…her best friend…

Cassie looked at me with tear-filled eyes.

"Dakota, I –," she stammered.

I held up my hand to silence her.

Mrs. Charlotte, Lena's mama, reached out and touched my arm.

"Scum of the fuckin' earth!" Mr. Felder accused, pointing a long, callused finger at Jace.

"Brett, we are in a church!" His wife scolded him. He pressed his lips together in a thin line.

I locked eyes with my best friend of over twenty years, his expression confirming what I already knew to be true. Without a thought, I swung, connecting nicely with his perfectly chiseled jaw. He crumpled to the floor in a heap. The gasps from those around me assured me this wasn't some weird dream.

This is actually fuckin' happening.

Stepping over the lump of a groom, I hauled ass to my truck, my now ex-fiancé chasing behind me.

"Dak, please!" She pleaded. "Just listen! I can explain!"

"My best friend, Cassie? No, fuck that, YOUR best friend? Where the fuck is Lena?" I demanded.

I can say fuck, right? I'm in the parking lot, not the actual church.

My anger intensified when she didn't immediately answer me.

"Where the fuck is Lena?" I asked again, the tone in my voice daring her to ignore me.

"I- I don't know. She caught us and she… she left," she sobbed.

Without another word, I jumped in my truck and hauled ass out of the parking lot.

Jolene

"Invalid code entry. Please see owner."

Motherfucker!

I tried another number combination.

"Invalid code entry. Please see owner."

I swear before the Lord, this is some fuck shit.

Another code combination.

"Invalid code entry. Please see owner."

What the fuck is the code!?!?!

Pulling my phone from my cleavage in the trashiest way possible, I weighed my options. Realizing that the only workable one was texting Dak or his daddy for it, I slid my iPhone back to its hiding spot between double and d.

I'll jump this fence if I have to before I call anyone that is at that damn church.

Ignoring the fact that the fence was well over twelve foot tall, I tried one last four-digit code. The gate's engine, or whatever it is that makes the fucker move, roared to life and the bitch slid to the left.

Jackpot! Dumbass fuckin' fence.

Ignoring the fact that the train to my gown was hung up, I slammed my car in drive. The tires on my Chevy Tahoe screeched on the loose, mountain gravel.

The old log cabin looked beautiful, and I fucking hated it.

Fuck honeymoon destinations that wind up not being used as honeymoon destinations.

The large, three-story cabin truly was beautiful. Having been friends with Dakota since we were young, we've spent so many summers, winters, and all things in between up here. His daddy nicknamed Jace, Dakota, Cassie and myself The Foolish Four because we've been in trouble up here more times than I can count. There was the time when we accidentally flooded the family room after overfilling the hot tub and leaving the back, sliding glass door open. There was the time we broke the railing off the balcony upstairs because we all got drunk and decided we wanted to repel down the side of the house. There was the time we tried to go full on Kevin McCallister and sled down the banister, through the side door, and down the side of the mountain hill, only to rip half the banister off the wall.

It's a wonder Big Jake didn't ban us from the cabin.

The cabin had been in the Clayton family for four generations and was as classic as it could possibly be, with only small tidbits of modern living. We finally convinced Dakota's daddy, known to most everyone as Big Jake, to add WiFi a few years ago because we are all adults now and loved escaping here to work. The Verizon router and the newly renovated kitchen and bathroom were the only real upgrades, everything else was put in and kept the same way that Great Grand Daddy Clayton had built it.

Fuck, please let there be firewood chopped already. I'm not in a calm enough mindset to be trusted with an ax, or an ex, right now.

As I stared at the cabin, fresh pain flooded my veins.

You not only fucked up my life, my wedding day, and my friendship with my best friend, Jace, you fucked up my happy place and every good memory I've had since I was a teenager.

I jumped out my SUV, the gravel penetrating my bunny slippers.

Fuck, I hadn't even put on my damn high heels when I ran the fuck outta there.

I stomped to the front porch, my bunny ears bouncing with every step. A moment of panic washed over me as I remembered I didn't have the keys. Dak was going to give them to us at the reception.

Fortunately, I knew where the hide-a-key was hidden. One twist of the old key and the front door swung open. The smell of time, familiarity, and cedar smacked me in the face.

The feeling of being at home was too much and my anger turned into ache.

Dakota

"Get the fuck outta my way!"

Apparently, everybody has somewhere to be at two fuckin' thirty on the second Saturday in December.

The ride to the mountain house has never seemed so long. Everyone seemed to be out for a joy ride, none of them with the same urgency I'm feeling to get the fuck out of Creek's Edge.

Cassie and Jace. Fucking.

I never saw the signs. There were no indicators.

How could there have been, Dakota? We were always with Jace and Jolene. It was easy for them to hide it because neither Lena nor I would have batted an eye about them talking.

Traffic finally thinned out enough that I could flirt a little harder with the other side of the speed limit.

God, if you're feelin' any sympathy for ya boy today, please don't let there be one of those God's Special People on top of that hill.

I guess He decided to throw me a bone because when I topped the hill at 85mph and there wasn't a Georgia State Patrol in sight.

Grabbing my phone, I dialed Lena's number. A moment later, her southern accent came on the line, pleasantly reminding me to leave a voicemail or text her because she hates to talk on the phone.

She cut her damn phone off.

As I sat mine back on the center console, it started to vibrate. A quick glance confirmed what I already knew before I looked down. It was Cassie for the umpteenth time, her contact photo from the day I proposed glaring up at me.

"Don't give a fuck about anything you have to say, Cassie," I spoke out loud to no one but myself.

The phone came to a silent rest, only to start dancing for me again a second later.

Let's take a page out of Lena's book.

I held the wheel with one hand and held down the button on the side of my phone with the other.

There you go, Cass. Now, you can explain to my voicemail why you deemed it necessary to fuck my best friend.

Traffic continued to thin out as I came up on the exit I needed to take to get to Belleview. Only five more miles and I'd be at the mountain house, drowning every memory of this day in a bottle of whiskey.

I'm definitely gonna need to stop at the liquor store before I get there because it's going to take more than a bottle to cure the pain in my knuckles and more persistently, my fuckin' chest.

Jolene

Thank goodness for the forever stocked liquor bar.

I made a mental note to thank Big Jake the next time I saw him.

I stomped from the bar to the sliding glass back door, the train of my dress snagging on every piece of furniture in between. Twisting off the top of the bottle and tossing it across the room, I tilted the room temperature bottle of Jack Daniels to my lips and chugged.

It burned all the way down my throat, settling into a fiery puddle in the pit of my stomach. The pain was no match to what I was already feeling so I took another swig. The burn was equally persistent but welcomed.

I need to text Mama and Daddy before I get shitfaced and let them know I'm alive.

My iPhone sang me a tune as it roared to life, missed call after missed call popping up in my notifications. Along with the intentionally missed calls, dozens of text alerts screamed at me. Cassie, Jace, Mama, Daddy, my cousin, Laura, my uncle, some work friends, some of my regular customers from my side hustle in candle making, my neighbor, one of the firefighter's wives.

Everyone dies famous in a fuckin' small town.

Ignoring every existing text, I created a group chat with my Mama and Daddy.

I'm alive and safe. I'm at Belleview with a bottle of Jack Daniels. Staying here, at least for tonight, and will not be driving. Or getting in the hot tub, Daddy, so don't worry I won't drown. Turning my phone off but if you need me, you have the cabin's house phone number. Love y'all.

Without bothering to see what anyone else had to say in my messages, and ignoring the incoming call from Jace, I squeezed the volume and home button on my phone until the screen went black.

Fuck you, fuck her, and fuck all this.

I took another gulp of whiskey, the deliciousness extinguishing the fire it had originally started. I felt my face heat up, a sure sign that the drink was doing its job correctly.

Eventually it won't hurt, or I'll pass out and do this again tomorrow.

I wanted to go out on the back patio and scream until my lungs forced me to stop, but my clumsiness combined with the whiskey stopped me.

Last thing I need is my parents finding my body down the side of the mountain, in this dumbass wedding dress, no less.

The reminder that I was still wearing the strapless Vera Wang forced me to look down – and take another swallow.

The dress that was once the most beautiful thing I'd ever seen in my life suddenly looked like a rag on my pale skin. The beautiful satin that had felt so luxurious against my skin only hours before now felt like it was squeezing the life from my body, but I couldn't be bothered to take it off. There was too much whiskey to be drunk.

You probably can't get this bitch off anyways. There's like a hundred fuckin' buttons down the back of this damn thing.

Instead of worrying about the satin straitjacket I'd paid out the ass for, I plopped down on the couch and wailed.

Wailed for the loss of my best friend, wailed for the loss of my future husband, and wailed for everything I had planned for my future.

Through my screams, I heard the front door slam.

Jace found me.

Dakota

What the fuck is that noise?

Flinging open the front door, I rushed inside the cabin.

In the living room on the leather sofa sat a poofy white cupcake and she was screaming into the oblivion.

Lena. Halle-fuckin' lujah.

She stopped screaming when she saw me, but she jumped to her feet in surprise.

The unsteadiness she had on her feet told me she and I had similar coping methods.

"Dakota! You scared the fuck outta me!"

"You scared me! Where the fuck is your car!?"

She looked at me like I'd lost my mind.

"It's outside?"

No, the fuck it's not.

"No, it's not."

"Well, I didn't walk here Dak." She rolled her eyes.

Well, no shit, Sherlock.

"Where did you park?" I asked, trying to keep my patience.

"Out- fuckin-side, bro! In the fuckin' yard!!"

Now it was my turn to roll my eyes.

Opening the front door, I stuck my head out. No Chevy Tahoe to speak of.

Dear Lord, please don't let her car be down the side of the fuckin' mountain.

Directing my tone towards the living room where the blushing bride was guzzling from an ancient bottle of whiskey, I spoke calmly.

"Lena, your car isn't out there, doll."

Exasperated, she stalked towards me, her feet not nearly as dedicated to the mission as her mind. As she reached the doorway, she tripped on her dress, causing me to reach out to steady her.

"I'm FINE," she declared, angrily. I let go of her arm.

"My car is right THERE, Dakota!" She pointed to the woodline.

She parked in the damn woods?

"Why did you park in the damn woods?"

"I didn't want anyone to find me but look-a- fuckin' here!" She spat, venom dripping from her voice.

I forgot how spicy this girl can get.

"It's my cabin," I pointed out. "I came here for the same reason you did."

Her expression softened as the realization hit her that she wasn't the only one suffering.

"I'm sorry, Dak." She spoke softly before extending the bottle of Jack to me.

Holding up the brown paper bag in my right hand, I shook my head. "Brought my own, girlie pop."

I made my way across the room and sat not one, but two bottles of Jack Daniels on the bar top.

"Damn, you were prepared. It didn't even occur to me to stop and get more. I just knew we had left some up here last time we were here, and I was banking on it," she explained.

"Yeah, well, the last few hours have definitely taught me to not expect a goddamn thing just because I know it's supposed to be. Want a shot?"

Jolene

I watched Dakota pour himself a shot into one of the glasses they kept in the cabinet.

Look at him being all professional with it while I'm swilling from the bottle like a neanderthal.

"Want a shot?"

I held up my bottle before tipping it to my lips.

The burn was back, evidence that it had been too long since my last gulp.

"We need to eat something, Lena."

I wrinkled my nose in disgust.

"Yeah, no. This works." Another gulp.

Shrugging, he turned up his own bottle.

Thank you for abandoning the shotglass, Mr. Fancy Pants.

I threw myself down on the sofa, nearly sliding off as the satin struggled to grip onto the leather.

"Please don't break your damn neck. Why are you still wearing that?"

Because I didn't have the fucks to change, bro.

"I hadn't been here but a few minutes when you busted up in here like the fuckin' feds. Whiskey was more important than wardrobe," I pointed out.

"You look like a fuckin' cupcake," he muttered before turning his bottle up again.

First of all, rude. Second of all, I paid a lot of money to look like a fuckin' cupcake and I'll fight you with one titty out and the law on the way.

"I like my dress, thank you very fuckin' much. I don't give a fuck if you don't."

He looked shocked.

"I didn't say I didn't like it. You look beautiful."

My heart lurched and I felt the tears threaten.

"Thanks, Dak."

"Anytime, Loo. Do me a favor?"

A favor? Now?

"What?" I snapped.

"Can you cool your jets a little? Same team, girl, same team."

My scowl softened.

He's hurting too, Lena. His world was just ripped away from him, too.

"I'm sorry. I know you're hurting, too," I apologized.

With the bottle to his lips, he nodded, chugging down an amount that would have left me unable to walk.

He threw himself down next to me on the couch.

"Did you have any signs?"

With new tears threatening, I shook my head.

His sympathetic blue eyes washed over me.

"Me, neither. How did you find out?"

Taken aback by his question, I tried to find my voice.

"I had just gotten to the church and Mama wanted to go find Daddy to fix his tie, but she couldn't find Cassie," I rambled. "I told her she was probably in her mama's office, so I went to look and…"

"And what?" He demanded.

I sighed. "And he had her bent over her mama's desk. Her damn maid of honor dress was hiked up around her hips. His tuxedo pants were around his ankles."

He shook his head in disgust.

"Sounds like a goddamn bad porno."

Nodding in agreement, I took another swig.

He reached over and touched my satin covered knee.

"I'm sorry, Lena."

The look in his eyes broke the dam behind mine and fresh sobs washed over me. He pulled me into his arms and let me cry, doing his best to disguise some tears of his own.

I guess if you're going to be brokenhearted, the best way to do it is with your buddy and some booze.

Dakota

"When did we cut those back on?" I slurred.

Jesus, Dak, you sound like you're talkin' in fuckin' cursive.

"I had to make a post on Facebook for the company!"

Why?

"The bank will still be open on Monday, Loo. Cassie didn't fuck around on my dad."

She shook her head, her face crinkled with irritation.

"The fuckin' candle page, Dak. Why the fuck would I make a post for the bank?"

Why would you do it for your candle company?

"Why do it for the candle page? What did you even say?" I snatched her phone out of her hand.

No taking orders for now. Finance fgucked bestie. Love yall

Oh my god, how the fuck do I delete that?

"Lena, you can't post that," I lectured as I pressed delete.
"Everyone will know anyways, and no one will be expecting you to take orders right now."

She stomped over to the back door and slid it open. The blast of cold air hit me like a knife. She shivered as she stood in the doorway, staring out into the dark mountains. Spying the tuxedo jacket I had long abandoned over the back of the couch, I grabbed it and stumbled across the room to drape it across her shoulders.

You'd be warmer if you'd take off this goddamn dress, Lena Loo.

I stood behind her to make sure she didn't fall. I was definitely feeling the side effects of all the whiskey we had wiped away and I have about a hundred pounds and six inches on her so there's no way she wasn't feeling it, too.

From the couch, her phone wailed, the sound too aggressive to be a text. Remembering that it had made the same sound a few minutes ago, I decided to check it out.

NWS Columbia has issued a Winter Storm Warning for your area. Heavy snow accumulation expected. 6-8 inches. Threats include black ice, dangerous travel, and power outages.

"Well, that's fuckin' terrific," I muttered.

Lena spun around. "What?"

I held out her phone as if she could read the small print from three feet away.

"I didn't bring my binoculars, Dak. Just fuckin' read it," she commanded, her southern accent even thicker from exasperation.

"Basically, we are likely gonna be stuck here."

She didn't bat an eye.

"We are under a winter storm warning and they're saying there will be black ice and up to eight inches of snow," I continued.

Still no reaction.

"Lena? Snow. Ice. Eight inches.

"I wasn't planning on leaving anyways," she pointed out.

Fair point.

"That's true." I tossed her phone back on the sofa.

"Besides, way less than eight inches fucked my world up today so I wouldn't mind seeing what a few more inches can do."

It may have been her accent, it may have been the booze, but whatever it was made my cock stir beneath my tuxedo pants.

Jolene

I realized what I'd said after I'd already said it. Honestly, this is far too common with me. I don't think before I speak and then I'm as shocked as everyone else about what comes out of my mouth.

"What I mean is –"

He laughed. "You're fine, Lena."

Are you laughing at me?

"Don't laugh at me."

Pressing his lips together, he did his best to hold back.

He stood and walked towards me, revealing more of himself that was refusing to be held back.

Oh my God.

"Close the door, Lena. It's fuckin' freezing." Grabbing my arm, he pulled me from the doorway and slid the door closed. "Why don't we get you out of that wedding dress?"

I eyed him curiously.

Excuse me, Lt.?

Exasperated, he shook his head. "Not like that! You're freezing, the damn train of that thing keeps getting' caught on everything, it's about to fuckin' snow and you need more clothes on than that!" He ran his fingers through his short hair.

He's so funny when he's flustered.

"My clothes are in my car," I admitted.

"And your car is in bum fuck Egypt because someone thought she could hide her car at a location that she was already supposed to be at today and even if she hadn't been supposed to be here, this is still the number one place anyone would look!"

"You didn't see my car or know I was here until you were inside," I pointed out.

"Fair point, but it's cold as fuck and because I'm a gentleman, I'm about to walk two hundred yards in temperatures that are negative fuck you because you can't wear that all night."

I shook my head. "I can go get it. I'm not helpless." I started walking towards the front door.

Within seconds, he was on my arm, pulling me backwards. "In that dress? With this wind? You'll get your ass blown down the mountain. I'll go."

"The wind isn't even that bad yet!" I hollered, irritated.

"Ok, I was being nice. What I should have said was 'In that dress, with this wind, and your clumsiness, and Jack Daniels?'"

Picking up a throw pillow from the couch, I threw it at him. He caught it with ease, smiling from ear to ear as he propped it back where it belonged.

"I'll go, Lena. Seriously, it's cold."

Nodding, I conceded.

I didn't want to walk out there in the dark anyways.

He opened the front door and stepped onto the porch. Before the door could even close behind him, he was walking back in the living room.

"Yeah, fuck that, you can wear something of mine. That wind is a bitch and a half." He shivered as he spoke. He unzipped his bag, grabbed a pair of sweatpants and a t-shirt, and tossed them to me.

Without thinking, I lifted the clothes and inhaled. They smelled of Dak and expensive body wash.

"Are you sniffing my clothes? They're clean. I keep an extra bag in the truck in case I need a change of clothes while I'm at the station," he explained.

I blushed, embarrassed. "They smell good. I was trying to figure out if I could tell what laundry detergent you use," I lied.

"Tide. Now, go change."

Ummm…

"I can't."

"Why?" He looked confused.

I spun around. "There's about a billion fuckin' buttons and I can't undo them by myself."

His eyes widened a fraction, and he reached for his bottle of Jack. He tossed a few gulps back before nodding at me.

"Ok, let's see if I can get you out of the dress."

Dakota

Why do wedding dresses have so many goddamn buttons? Why can't they put a fuckin' zipper back here or something?

I had unbuttoned about thirty buttons and there was still more to go.

"They really want to put a damper on the wedding night with all these damn buttons," I muttered under my breath.

She laughed. "Yeah, but turns out, there's an even better way to fuck it up. Groom rails maid of honor who just so happens to be engaged to the best man!"

Her body shook from either sobs or laughter, I couldn't be sure from behind. The last button was right above her ass, and I made easy work of unfastening it. As I stood back to admire my handy work, I noticed her bare back was covered in goosebumps.

"Lena, grab the t-shirt and put it on."

She didn't move but the laughter stopped.

Stepping around the white enormity that was her wedding train, I realized she was silent because she was testing her ability to chug a third of a bottle of whiskey down in one gulp.

"Chug! Chug! Chug!"

Why am I cheering this on? She's half naked.

She finished the bottle and held it up triumphantly before abandoning the empty bottle on the bar top. She looked so proud of herself that I couldn't help but smile.

"Good girl."

She stopped mid-shuffle to the bathroom.

Uh oh, she's gonna vomit.

"What did you just say?" she demanded.

"Good girl," I enunciated.

"Don't say that," she warned.

The fuck?

"I'll do what I want, but for curiosity's sake, why?"

"Because I said so."

I rolled my eyes.

"Go change, Lena." I chugged from my half empty bottle of whiskey.

Turning around, she continued her shuffle with one arm holding the strapless, snow colored garment in place.

"Good girl."

Spinning back around, she dropped her arm, and the dress went with it. She stood before me in nothing but a lacy, white thong with a garter belt, some sheer thigh white stockings and some sort of lacy, flowery nipple covers.

Fuck me running.

I had seen her in a bikini millions of times.

Hell, I had probably seen her naked before. We've all been friends since we were kids, and we all used to go skinny dipping all the time, but that was back when I had no reason to be looking so I didn't.

You shouldn't be looking now either, Dipshit.

We stood in silence, her staring at me, defiantly, and me staring at her, deliberately.

One of us has to speak.

"Do you need help?"

Yeah, that helped nothing and sounded more suggestive than anything else.

"Nope, I've decided I'm going to get in the hot tub," she proclaimed before wobbling to the back door.

You're what? The hot tub?

"Lena, you've been drinking and it's –"

"And I have a firefighter here that saves lives for a living that probably won't let me drown."

What the…

"Of course, I'm not going to let you drown but it's too fuckin' cold to get in that hot tub," I reminded her gently.

"Guess I better see what I can do to keep myself warm then," she winked.

That Jack Daniels smacked the logic all out of her.

Walking like a newborn deer, she stepped out onto the back deck and began peeling off her stockings.

Take your ass outside before she falls over the fuckin' railing.

"Lena, seriously, it's too fuckin' cold." The wind was brutal, cutting through the thin fabric of my monkey suit with ease.

Ignoring me, she climbed into the bubbly water, the only thing between her and I was the distance, the hot tub wall, and a lacy piece of dental floss.

Leave room for Jesus, Dak, leave room for Jesus.

"You gonna get in?"

No.

"I reckon I am because your drunk ass didn't give me much choice," I griped.

She laughed.

I peeled down to my boxers. Her laughter grew louder, echoing throughout the back deck and the open yard.

It's such an ego boost for a woman to be, literally, cackling as you strip in front of her.

"What's so damn funny?" I demanded. "Don't even say nothin' smart because it's about 18° out here and you decided it was the right time to strip and fuckin' swim!"

Her laughter only intensified, alternating between a snort and sounds of a walrus.

Ignoring her, I climbed in the warm water. As much as I hated to admit it, it really felt great in contrast to just standing around outside underneath Jack Frost's nutsack.

"Lena! Stop and breathe, fuck!"

She stopped immediately, tears of laughter on her freckled cheeks.

"What is so damn funny?"

Hanging her head, she spoke softly. "I forgot that the panties I have on… I forgot that…they're dissolvable."

What?

"What do you mean?"

Even with the dimmed lighting from the living room, I could see her blush.

"They're dissolvable! I ordered them online from some place called The Brazen Bride and when they get wet, as ALL PANTIES SHOULD ON A WEDDING NIGHT THAT GOES ACCORDING TO PLAN, they dissolve."

I couldn't get two brain cells to rub together to get a spark.

"I'm naked under the water, Dakota, except for these pasties which I'm fairly certain will be floating soon because the water is going to deactivate the sticky pad thing."

Lord, if you're testing me, I'm weak.

"Oh, okay."

We sat in the hot tub in silence. Tilting her head back, she lowered herself up to her neck and stared up at the night sky.

A single tear that even half a bottle of Jack Daniels couldn't prevent, rolled down her cheek.

The good friend in me wanted to hug her, to comfort her, to make sure she knew she didn't have to go through this alone, but the respectful man that knew she was naked, and I absolutely couldn't touch her at this moment, refrained.

"Lena?" I asked gently.

She turned to look at me but didn't speak.

"It's his loss, you know."

Nodding, she spoke quietly. "It's hers, too."

From beneath the water, I felt her grab my hand.

"I don't know what to do now. I will have to move back in with Mama and Daddy until I can buy a house, I have to figure out how to get all my shit from his house, I have to change my address, change my ID," she explained needlessly.

"None of that has to be done tonight, Lena Loo. Or even tomorrow. If you need me to, I'll go get your stuff from his house and if he has something to say about it, I'll rock his shit again."

She sat straight up in the water, giving me an unbridled look of her large chest. Her nipples hardened at the sudden exposure to the cold December air.

"Again? You hit Jace?"

Not as many times as I should have.

"Yes."

"What did he say when you hit him?" she interrogated.

"Ow?"

She shot me a glare.

"I don't know what he said, Lena, or if he said anything at all. He hit the floor. I stepped over him like the piece of shit he is and left."

Her eyes widened.

"Where was Cassie when all this was happening?"

You really want a full recap while you're completely naked in the hot tub, shitfaced, and in the middle of a winter storm warning?

"She was right there. I was in the room where all the groomsmen were hanging out and I heard hollerin'. It was your daddy. I went down the hall to see what the fuss was about and when I got down there and asked, he told me to ask my girlfriend."

She didn't speak but her eyes urged me on.

"I didn't even notice Cassie was there at first. I heard your daddy saying something about your best friend and when he told me to ask her, that's when I noticed her," I recalled. "When I looked at her, I just knew. She had mascara on her cheeks, she was standing between your daddy and Jace. I could just tell. So, I decked him and left."

"We are goin' to be the laughingstock of town," she remarked bitterly.

"No, we won't. If anything, we will get the sympathetic head tilts for a little while, but why would we get laughed at?" I was confused.

"They're going to say we should have known; that we should have noticed."

"Well, whoever 'they' are, they can kiss my ass. It never occurred to me to question the morals of my best friend, and I know it never occurred to you, either."

She nodded, the fresh tears she had been fighting back spilling down her cheeks.

Without thinking, I yanked her hand, pulling her to my side. As I put my arm around her, she rested her cheek against my chest, sobs wracking her slender body.

The whiskey abandoned me in that moment, and I felt the tears I didn't want to cry, colliding with her messy bridal curls.

Jolene

I'm naked in a hot tub with my fiancé's.... er... ex-fiancé's... best friend and my best friend's... ex best friend's... fiancé... ex-fiancé...

I don't know how long we sat like that. The minutes that ticked by seemed like hours. We both ignored the fact that my tits were pressed against his chest and that his cock was hard as a rock and swaying from the hot tub current. We both ignored all the things we should have been noticing if it was a different time, different circumstances, and a different person.

The whiskey I felt so stubbornly in my veins when I dropped the wedding dress may as well have been back in the bottle. Knowing how I found out was one thing that kept replaying in my head over and over but hearing him explain how he found out… it made it so real. I wasn't imagining this. It wasn't a dream I was going to wake up from.

My best friend and the man that I planned my life with are having an affair.

The pain suddenly felt so fresh, so suffocating that it sucked the air from my lungs. I gasped, willing the open air to replenish me, but my attempt was futile.

"Are you ok?"

I gasped, a plea for my lungs to find some act right.

"Lena!" He pulled me into his lap and shook me.

Steadying myself on his shoulders, I tried to inhale, coughing as my body rejected perfectly good oxygen.

"Lena, you're having a panic attack," he spoke calmly. "In through the nose, out through the mouth. Slowly."

Following his instructions, I only failed a little, a small puff of air finally making its way in.

"That's it. Slowly. Find a focal point and breathe. In through your nose, out through your mouth."

His fingertips caressed my back as he consoled me, his mind completely oblivious to my naked pussy pressing against him.

Breathing slowly the way he demanded, the burn in my lungs finally began to dissipate, the invisible hold on my windpipe, vanishing.

"Good girl, keep breathing," he cajoled. "You're doing great, Loo."

My breathing slowly regulated, my heartbeat following suit.

As my respiratory system went on about business, whatever system it is that controls the embarrassment ramped up.

"I'm sorry. I was thinking about everything that happened and reliving it and I suddenly felt like I couldn't take a breath."

His fingertips danced from my waist to my shoulder blades.

"You don't have to apologize, but are you okay? How's your chest feeling?"

Instinctively, we both looked down. My chest was pressed against his, my full tits flush against his tattooed chest.

"It, uh, feels warm," I stuttered.

He laughed so hard his body shook, the vibration rippling against every sensitive part of my body.

"Warm on the inside or on the outside?"

"The outside. The inside feels normal."

Nodding, he released the grip he had on me.

He's telling you to get off, dumbass.

Humiliated, I slid across him, feeling all the forecasted eight inches against a place that had never seen that many inches at once.

Bitch, you need more whiskey and a wet dream.

Dakota

Holy fuck.

I don't know what was scarier, hoping and praying Lena didn't die in this hot tub from a panic attack, or hoping and praying my little lieutenant didn't make his way through that little convenient opening in the front of my boxers to make contact with her bare pussy.

On the built-in bench next to me, she shivered.

"You're freezing, aren't you?"

She nodded.

"I'll go grab us some towels. Wait here."

Doing my best to make sure the tent I was pitching was out of sight, I climbed out of the hot tub and scurried inside.

I'm blaming the entire reaction of the southern hemisphere on grief induced insanity.

Grabbing two towels from the linen closet in the hallway, I dripped my way back outside.

"Look alive, Lena Loo. Here's your towel!" I sat it on the edge of the hot tub before turning around.

Please do not slip and fall getting out. Please do not slip and fall getting out.

Feeling unbelievably thankful for the absence of a thud, I dried myself off.

"Are you covered?"

"Yes, wrapped up. Where did you put your sweatpants?" Her teeth chattered as snow began to fall around us.

"They're on the couch. Go get warm."

I followed her into the house, grateful for the blast of heat that smacked me in the face as I crossed the threshold.

The sound of the bathroom door shutting calmed my frayed nerves as I rifled through my bag for something to put on.

"Did I take the only thing you had to wear?"

Fuck, she is quiet as a church mouse.

"No, I have more, I'm just trying to find it. Are you warmed up?" I glanced over my shoulder.

She was standing there, her thin body swimming in my clothes. Her face had been scrubbed free of all her wedding makeup and her messy pinned hair tumbled around her elbows in haphazard curls.

She is beautiful. Jace really played his fuckin' self.

She nodded.

"Good."

After finally finding another pair of sweatpants and a t-shirt, I hauled ass to the bathroom to change.

Fuck, boxers. I forgot boxers.

"Commando, it is," I spoke softly to myself.

"Did you say something?" she called out from the other side of the door.

Not as soft spoken as I thought, apparently.

I opened the door and stepped out, shaking my head.

"I was just thinkin' out loud," I clarified. "Are you hungry? I'm not sure what we have here but Dad usually keeps it pretty well stocked and up to date."

She shook her head.

"You need to eat, Loo," I scolded gently. "I'm going to make you something and I really hope you'll try a few bites, if for no other reason than to shut me up."

Curling up on the couch, she pulled a blanket over herself, trying and failing to hide the smile on her face.

I rummaged around the kitchen, looking for anything I could turn into something. As luck would have it, there was a few pounds of frozen hamburger meat in the deep freezer with a label in my dad's messy handwriting from only three weeks ago and a few cans of tomato sauce in the cabinets. If I could find some pasta, we would be firing on all cylinders. After finally finding everything that I needed, I fired up the gas stove.

Nothing says happy failed wedding day like piss poor spaghetti with the other scorned party of the groom's hidden affair.

Jolene

The smell of garlic and tomatoes flooded my nostrils.

Damn, maybe I am hungry.

Companionable silence stretched across the living room. I guess one of the perks of being friends as long as we have, we didn't feel the need to fill the silence with idle chitchat.

"Dakota?"

He jerked his head up from whatever it was he was chopping on the kitchen counter.

"Hmmm?"

"How long do you think it was going on?"

Sighing, he set down the knife and stepped around the island.

"I dunno. I like to think it couldn't have been very long because it hurts less that way, but I guess it could have been happening for years."

He walked over to the sofa.

"Why would she accept your proposal? And why would he ask me to marry him if they wanted each other?" I questioned, unable to disguise the pain in my voice.

Ruffling my hair, he shook his head. "I wish I had an answer for that, Loo. Maybe for the thrill? The adrenaline?"

Surely, they didn't tear our fuckin' world apart over some goddamn adrenaline.

"Adrenaline?"

"Yeah. Jace is an adrenaline junkie. You kinda have to be in our line of work."

Adrenaline from fighting fire isn't the same as nailing your girl's bestie, Dak.

"I know, I know, it's not the same thing," he retorted, seemingly reading my thoughts. "I'm just saying he likes a good thrill. As far as Cassie is concerned, I have no idea. Hell, I have no idea if that's why he did it either, I'm just spit balling." He sighed.

"But how is that a thrill? Hurting people?" I whined.

"Because they don't see it that way. They see it as it's forbidden, and the thrill comes from doing something they shouldn't be and then there's the skirting around, so they don't get caught," he explained. "The rush of it is as rewarding as the outcome."

He walked back into the kitchen.

"I've never experienced a rush that made me lose me fuckin' mind," I announced. "I hope she doesn't think she's getting' a price. I had to use my fuckin' vibrator to make myself cum after we were done sometimes!"

Dakota dropped the spoon he was holding.

Well, well, apparently the whiskey has decided to remind me I drank a fuckton of it."

"You had to use… okay, then," he stammered.

Now would be an excellent time to shut the fuck up, Jolene.

"Sorry, too much information. Whiskey makes me a motormouth."

"You're fine. I'm sorry you had to DIY in your love life," he responded, choking back a laugh.

"I'm glad you're amused," I snapped.

He stopped stirring the sauce, complete and utter seriousness blanketing his face.

"No, I meant it. I'm sorry you've never had an experience where he had you climbin' the goddamn walls."

Heat unfurled deep inside me.

Lena, this is Dakota. Go to bed and wake up tomorrow to whatever fresh hell awaits.

Or you could play with fire…

"Make me climb the walls."

Dakota

What the fuck did she just say?

"Don't ask for something unless you're damn sure you want it," I warned.

She stood up from the sofa, peeling my t-shirt over her head as she rose.

"Lena...," I threatened, stalking towards her.

Slowly, with determined blue eyes, she pushed my sweatpants down her thighs, her long, blonde curls sweeping across her huge tits as she moved.

My breath hitched in my throat at the sight of her.

You're a dumbass motherfucker, Jace.

As we stood there, eyes locked, uncertainty and embarrassment fluttered across her face.

"Come over here," I demanded, my voice low.

Clearly surprised but obedient, she came towards me.

Any ounce of self-control I had evaporated the second she was at arm's length.

Grabbing her by the back of her neck, I tangled my fingers in the blonde waves at the base of her hairline and tugged, forcing her to look me in the eye.

"Lena….," I warned once more, pleading for her to tell me to stop and pleading for her to tell me to keep going.

Encircling my neck with her tiny palms, she pulled my mouth down to meet hers.

This is the part where my PASS device would go off.

Her lips were plump and juicy, marred with the subtle taste of Jack Daniels.

She moaned, a strained, deep sound that quaked me to my core.

I've got to stop this. Neither of us are in the place for this.

Sensing my hesitation, she pulled me closer, daring me to call her bluff as she slid her tongue between my lips. I welcomed her by opening my mouth deeper, encouraging her tongue to dance against my own.

Kissing her felt more dangerous than any fire I'd ever fought.

Needing more closeness, more passion, more *Lena*, I pulled her body into mine, every naked inch of her porcelain flesh searing me through my clothes. She kissed me with urgency, determination in her veins.

Fuck this.

Lifting with ease, I laid her back on the kitchen counter.

Shocked by my brazenness, every part of her turned crimson, embarrassment overtaking her.

"Tell me to stop, Lena." It wasn't a request. It was a plea.

She shook her head.

"Lena," I groaned. "Tell me to stop."

"I need this, Dak. I need you," she whimpered breathlessly.

I think I do, too.

Spreading her legs apart, I took in my new, unshielded view.

Her pussy was bare and glistening, a perfect match for my own throbbing situation. Her clit was damn near purple, swollen and barely peeking from beneath its hood. Using only my thumb, I stroked her, her body trembling against the counter in response.

"Mmm, do you like that, Lena?"

She nodded, suddenly looking more innocent than I'd ever seen her. I stopped my probing.

She propped up on her elbows, her eyes flashing.

"Can't finish the drill, Lt.?"

Ya know what...

Using both hands, I spread her pussy open, toying with every part I wanted against my tongue.

She smells so goddamn good.

Teasing her, I tapped on her fully exposed, throbbing clit.

"Dak!"

"Don't like that? What about this?" Using her own juices to guide my way, I traced the edge of her pulsating hot spot. She arched herself off the countertop, silently begging for more.

"God, I want to fuckin' taste you."

Aggressively and without warning, she grabbed my head and pressed it against her body.

If I'd ever sat back and imagined how incredible she would taste, it wouldn't have even come close to the real thing.

As she held me in place, my tongue explored every inch that I could reach before landing on her pulsing center. She ground her pussy against my lips, my tongue tormenting her every step of the way.

Make her climb the fuckin' walls, Dak.

Clamping my lips around her, I engulfed her clit into my mouth, flicking it with my tongue as I sucked. She began trembling beneath me and I knew that she was close. She pulled my head away, releasing the suction, only to push it back down a moment later.

"Pl-Please don't stop," she stammered, never releasing the hold she had on the back of my neck.

She screamed, a deep, guttural scream, as her orgasm washed over her. I increased the pressure behind the suction I had on her clit.

"Dak, too much. I- I – too much!"

Oh no, baby, you said you wanted to climb walls.

Determined to send her spiraling, I kept sucking and flicking, the pulse from within her vibrating against my tongue. She writhed from the counter, her moans echoing off the walls. Almost immediately, a gush of warm, sweet liquid flooded my mouth, my chin, and the counter beneath her.

Never have I ever wondered if Lena was a squirter but in this moment, I don't know how I ever lived without knowing it.

Jolene

Whatever that was… I've never felt that before.

"Are you okay?" He asked tentatively.

No, I'm not actually. I want to know why it's not always like that.

"I'm okay. That was…," I trailed off.

"That was what?" He questioned, arching an eyebrow at me.

I felt myself blushing.

"It was incredible," I admitted sheepishly.

I avoided his gaze, but I could feel him smiling down at me. Goosebumps skittered across my sweat-sheened body.

"I'm happy to hear it. Let's get you dressed," he instructed, pulling me gently to the sitting position.

Um, I would like to play with the railroad tie that I felt under me in the hot tub.

Before I could hop off the countertop, he held up the sweatpants, rolling them from the hem so I could slide my leg in.

Ok, I guess I'm getting dressed.

After sliding his pants over my hips, I hopped down, the old hardwood floor as cold as ice beneath my feet.

"I'm gonna go to bed, Lena. Take the master bedroom," he announced, starting down at the floor.

So, every relationship I held dear just went in the shitter today, huh?

"Okay. Thank you."

He nodded but said nothing before ascending the wooden staircase.

What the fuck did you just do, Jolene?

I know I've fucked up when my subconscious is calling me by my government name.

After grabbing my phone, I made my way up the stairs to the lonely bedroom at the end of the hall.

How many times have I slept in this room with Jace? How many times have I made love to him in this bed?

"A lot of times that don't make a fuck, Lena, because he was railing your best friend over the church secretary's desk," I argued with myself aloud.

I clapped my hands together and the bedside lamp came to life. Warm lighting illuminated the old cabin bedroom, the gleam on the vibrant old quilt on the bed reminding me of better days.

Jace wrapped that around me on graduation night after I drank entirely too much hunch punch and ended up throwing up over the balcony.

I pulled off the antique fabric, folded it, and laid it across the rocking chair in the corner.

You're going to freeze to death just covered up with the sheet.

I climbed under the thin fabric, ignoring how cold the room already felt.

The heater is on. You're just still moist from your nasty little tirade on Big Jake's kitchen counter!

The reminder that this cabin belonged to a man that was like a second daddy to me, a man who graciously gave me a job at his bank when I was just a senior in high school, a man who has allowed me to be part of his family for almost two decades and the disrespect I just…

What if he has fuckin' cameras, Lena?

I shot straight up in bed. *Cameras! Why the fuck didn't I think of the possibility of cameras when I was dropping the damn Vera Wang around my ankles!?*

Retrieving my phone from the nightstand, I cut it on, careful to avoid opening any of the billions of texts that Apple was screaming at me to open.

Scrolling through my contacts, I settled on Dakota's name.

Please tell me your daddy doesn't have cameras downstairs.

I pressed send.

I waited but a text from him never came. Several others popped on through from various people and mainly, Jace, but nothing from Dak Clayton.

Go wake him up, bitch.

But I couldn't. Not after what happened. Big Jake probably didn't have cameras.

Yeah, because what billionaire doesn't have cameras.

"But Big Jake isn't the flashy kind. You'd never have known he has money if you didn't know, and this isn't his main home. It's a vacation home," I reasoned with myself.

You have lost your entire fuckin' mind, Lena.

Switching my phone back off, I laid it on the nightstand.

He has his phone cut off, dumbass.

The silence of the dimly lit room was deafening.

I don't think I've ever been in this house where it's so quiet.

I stared at the pictures on the wall. Our senior class picture that we took on the back lawn, a framed picture of Cassie and Dakota from their engagement session, a framed picture of Jace and me from ours, a picture of our Creek's Edge National Bank family, a picture of Baxter, Dakota's childhood dog. Years and years of memories were scattered across the old walls, reminding me that everything would be different now.

Where the fuck do you go from here, Lena?

Before I could answer myself, the room went pitch black.

Dakota

Aaaaand the power is out.

"Fuck!" I cursed aloud.

"Dak!"

Lena.

"Comin'!" I climbed out of bed and tried to feel my way to the door. My equilibrium was off from the rendezvous with Jack Daniels and then the rendezvous with Lena.

I'm sure the absolute pitch-black room isn't helping.

"What the fuck happened?" She demanded from a few doors down.

I banged my knee against the stair railing as I baby stepped down the hallway.

I told your drunk ass we were under a winter storm warning!

Finally feeling what I thought was her door frame, I spoke gently.

"Remember the winter storm I mentioned? Yeah, that causes power outages."

I rolled my eyes, knowing she couldn't see me.

"I know you're rolling your eyes," she called out from somewhere inside the dark master bedroom.

Chuckling, I crab walked into her room, only to have my shin connecting with some fuck ass old piece of furniture. "You sum' BITCH!"

She howled with laughter. "Your eyes haven't adjusted?"

Obviously fuckin' not.

"Yeah, Lena Loo, they did. I just decided that I was gonna pick tonight to identify as a fuckin' bumper car." More laughter.

Well, I guess that's better than cryin'.

I rubbed my eyes. They were finally adjusting to the darkness, just in time for me to notice she was sitting on the floor.

"Why are you on the floor?"

"When the lights went out, I tried to grab my phone to turn it on and use the flashlight to come find you, but I knocked it off. I was looking for it."

Always so damn clumsy.

"Well, I'm here now, but there's just one problem."

I could feel her judgmental stare even in the dark.

"Just one problem… that's some interesting math skills you have, Lieutenant Clayton."

Smartass.

"Ok, there's just one new problem."

"Better."

"The only two parts of the house with a fireplace are in here and downstairs," I pointed out. Silence hung between us.

"Okay?" She sounded confused.

"Yeah, the one downstairs will warm up the living room after a while but with half of the back wall being glass windows, I'm not sure how much it will help, and I don't want to waste firewood tonight. I can cut more tomorrow but tonight, we need to use what we have in the most efficient way," I explained.

"Okay…"

Why is she answering me like I'm stupid?

"What?" I snapped.

"I'm just not sure what the problem is…," she trailed off. "I mean, ideally, we would have more wood ready to go but I'm not understanding what you mean is the problem if that's not the problem."

"We are both gonna have to sleep in here to make sure we stay warm. This house is going to get cold quick, Lena."

What part of what I'm saying isn't making sense?

"Dakota," she spoke up, her voice brimming with amusement.

"What?"

"We've slept in the same bed a million times. I think we even fell asleep in the bathtub together on my 21st birthday because Cassie threw up in the bed and Jace passed out on the back porch.

She's right. Why did I feel weird pointing out that we would have to do it tonight?

I knew why, but I wasn't going to say it out loud.

Because the most delicious part of her is still on your lips.

"Yeah, that's true. I just didn't know if you wanted to be alone but you're gonna just have to deal with me for tonight." I tried to sound lighthearted, but my heart was thunder stomping in my chest.

"I think I'll survive," she promised. "However, we need to find my phone, unless you have yours, so we can see how to get downstairs to get wood and matches and all that good shit."

Fuck, I left mine on the dresser.

"I'll help you find yours."

After we found her phone, she switched it on, the bright light offering a temporary solution to the fact that we were basically in a cave. No sooner than it made it to her home screen, it started going off, ding after ding forcing us to remember all the shit we were trying to forget.

A mutual glance determined we weren't opening a single damn message on that phone, so I pulled her to her feet for her to guide us to the staircase.

Jolene

"Strike it on the brick, Dak."

"I know what I'm doin', Lena!" He snapped.

Obviously, which is why you've been trying to light this bitch for thirty minutes and I'm sitting here fuckin' shivering.

"I'm just sayin' the box is old, the strike patch thing isn't working," I pointed out.

"You do realize I play with fire, like for a living?"

"You put fire out. You extinguish the fire. I'm not doubting your capabilities in that perspective. Clearly, you've got a handle on it because my nipples are so hard, they could cut glass right now."

He huffed. "Fine, let's do it your way!" He dragged the long match up the side of the brick fireplace, a spark erupting immediately.

"Well, whaddaya know?" I teased sarcastically.

Shaking his head, he tossed the match into the oversized fireplace, the seasoned fatlighter helping to bring the logs to life.

"Ok, so you were right, and I was wrong," he admitted. "Thanks."

"Anytime, partner. You're used to puttin' out the fires, not startin' them."

Nodding, he rose to his feet. "Let's go to bed, Loo."

Wordlessly, I crawled in on the right side and he crawled in on the left, the smooth execution of muscle memory from climbing into bed with Jace and Cassie for all these years.

He must be used to sleeping on the left.

The room was completely silent except for the fire cracking and the wind roaring outside.

The companionable silence from earlier is suffocating now.

Rolling over to face him, I called out his name.

"Yes?"

Deep breaths

"About earlier… I shouldn't have…encouraged that. Started it, rather. I should have left well enough alone and stopped drinkin' when the room became swirly and I shouldn't have taunted you into doing something you didn't want to do," I rambled. "I'm sorry and I'd love it if we could forget it ever happened."

He stared at me, his blue eyes twinkling from the light of the fire.

"It wasn't just you. I know you felt how hard I was in the hot tub. Not braggin' but it had to be hard to ignore when I was pressing into you."

Oh yeah… he was hard. How had I forgotten?

"Yeah, what was that about?" I asked, doing my best to sound nonchalant.

"I'd like to be the guy that blames the liquor, but you know I'm more of a truth guy. You're sexy as fuck and you were naked in my hot tub because you went and bought some damn dissolvable drawstrings to wear on your ass."

Dissolvable drawstring is diabolical.

"You did not just say I'm sexy. That should be the absolute last way you see me. Remember that time I clogged the toilet at the party because y'all motherfuckers insisted we have taco bell before we went, and you took the blame for me?"

He wrinkled his nose. "That was absolutely in the top ten worst things my nostrils ever had to endure… and I'm a first responder."

I whacked him with a pillow.

"Just because we are close, it doesn't mean I'm too stupid to see that you're attractive, Lena. You've always been beautiful. I've never thought or said anything different. Just because I never thought of takin' you to bed before, it doesn't equate to blindness."

Just because he never thought of takin' me to bed…before.

"You said you never thought of taking me to bed before. Does that mean you're thinkin' about it now?"

"I'm in bed with you now," he pointed out.

I whacked him again.

"You know what I mean."

"Hand to God, I have never thought of touchin' you like that until earlier when it happened."

Me, neither.

"Yeah, I never thought of it, either. Not until that moment and you can be Abe Lincoln with your truthfulness, but I'm blaming the whiskey," I proclaimed.

He chuckled. "It wasn't the whiskey. We are both going through something that very few people can relate to. We are already close friends, we are stranded here together, and we are both feelin' like we weren't good enough for the person we planned to spend the rest of our lives with."

When I didn't speak, he went on. "It wasn't the healthiest of coping mechanisms, but it was fuckin' fantastic in that moment because we both felt whatever that goddamn feeling of comfort is that was ripped away from us today."

A very dirty coping mechanism…

"But you just said you hadn't ever looked at me that way?" He was confusing me.

"I hadn't." He confirmed. "Until you were standing naked in front of me."

"You've seen me naked a million times, Dakota."

He shot up in bed, exasperation radiating from his body. "I have but never after you've asked me to make you climb the goddamn walls, Lena!"

My face grew hotter than the fire.

"Dak, I'm –"

"Stop apologizing. You didn't force me. No, I had never thought about tasting your pussy before that moment, but I haven't stopped thinkin' about it since."

I'm sorry, what?

"I know it feels like we did something wrong. That's because of our character, but at the end of the day, I'm choosin' to look at it as, it made a shitty day a little less shitty. So, stop beatin' yourself up over it before I have to remind you again that it was worth every fuckin' second."

Dakota

Her mouth dropped open.

Exactly. Now, stop.

"I didn't know I could do that."

What?

"Do, what?"

Even with only the light from the fireplace flickering over us, I saw her blush a deep crimson.

"Squirt."

More blushing.

That man had the balls to fuck around on her with her best friend and couldn't make her squirt?

"Never?"

She shook her head. "We didn't do a lot of foreplay. I loved sucking his dick but, well, yeah."

"Well, yeah, what?" I demanded.

"I would suck his dick first, then he would eat me out for a few seconds and say he couldn't take it anymore and he wanted to be inside me," she explained, her voice bordering on a whisper.

The pang or irritation, or maybe even jealousy that burned in my gut, took me by surprise.

"That's just fuckin' lazy."

She shrugged her shoulders. "I thought maybe I tasted bad, but I don't understand how because you know how I am about showering."

I rolled my eyes. I can't even count how many times I've heard this girl say she was ready to take a shower.

"Well, let me be the one to clear that shit up right now. You taste incredible. Surprisingly sweet, actually."

"Why's that surprising?"

"Because you tasted unusually sweet. What fruit do you eat the most?"

"Pineapple," she answered, her confusion palpable.

"Makes sense."

"Yeah, that clarifies nothing. Anyways, all that to say, I didn't know I could do that so thank you for teaching me a new trick."

I chuckled. "Baby, you did that because of me. No other man will ever do it quite like I did to make you squirt like that and I'm not suggesting you start holding auditions."

Why do I feel so goddamn irritated?

"Holding auditions? What does that even mean?"

For fucks sake

"It means if you want to squirt like that again, you know where to find me. Don't go lookin' for me in any fuckin' body else."

She opened her mouth to speak but decided against it.

"What?" I snapped.

You need to calm the fuck down, man.

"You expect me to call you every time I want to get off? Yeah, that's not fuckin' happening."

The shy, somewhat inexperienced Lena was gone. Normal, bratty ass Lena had returned.

"Why the fuck not?" I demanded. "You seemed to enjoy yourself."

More blushing.

"So, you want me to shoot you a text and be like, 'Hey bud, how 'bout them Dawgs! Oh, I need to squirt, can you come over?'"

Is that what I'm saying? Goddamn, I'm so confused.

"Seems like a good arrangement, no?"

"No. What if I have things I want to do?"

Too fuckin' bad.

"Such as?"

"Suck start your fucking soul."

I choked on… nothing.

Did I just damn near die because I inhaled…oxygen?

I throbbed from beneath my Under Armour sweatpants.

"You know where to find it." *How witty, Dakota.*

Staring me in the eyes, she reached under the sheet, her small palm coming to rest on my waistband. Sliding her hand inside it, she paused, but not before her fingertips grazed every inch of my little lieutenant.

"Breathe, Dak," she teased. "I've barely touched you."

"In the last few hours, I've had your bare pussy pressing against me, your throbbing clit between my lips, and your sweet cum flooding my face. Pardon me for being worried about being a little trigger happy."

With a grin, she wrapped her hand around me, my hips bucking against her in surprise.

"You are a little trigger happy, aren't you?" She taunted me, pulling back the sheet to stare at my dick in her hand.

"You'd look so much cuter with something in your mouth."

She laughed, a deep laugh that echoed off the walls and jiggled her tits.

"Well, in case you need a visual."

Huh?

"What do you mean a vis – ahhh!"

Without warning, she deepthroated, the swollen head of my cock coming to rest just beyond her tonsils. "Lena, goddamn!"

She bobbled her head to push me further, her tongue tickling the nerve endings on the underside of my shaft.

"Oh, fuckkk."

She gagged and kept going, a free hand entering the game to massage my tender, aching balls.

She was unrelenting, torturous even, inflicting so much overstimulation that I was unable to speak. My hips were uncontrollable, lurching involuntarily in a manner that resembled fucking her throat. She moaned low in her throat, the small gesture rippling throughout my sensitive sack.

"Lena, I can't – I. Gonna cum." I managed, trying to pull her away by her hair. This only encouraged her efforts, and she opened her throat more to deepen her hold onto me.

"Lena, stop, I'm gonna cum, I can't. Let up. FUCK!"

My body shook unwillingly, the pleasure too damn much at once.

While closing her throat to mimic a swallow, she firmly but gently squeezed my balls.

The perfect level of pain and constriction were my undoing and with one final lurch, I erupted, shooting spurt after spurt down her extremely experienced throat.

What the FUCK was that?

Releasing her hold on me, she sat back on her heels, her beautiful face the epitome of amusement and triumph.

"Hey buddy?"

I made a sound that was nowhere near close to actual words, but I think it closely resembled a "huh?"

"How 'bout them Dawgs."

Jolene

Within two minutes, I heard him snoring.

And that's on a job well done.

I licked my lips proudly, savoring the taste he left behind.

After checking to see if I needed to add wood to the fire, I pulled the sheet up to my chin.

I can't believe I just had Dakota in my mouth.

I wouldn't say that I've always looked at him as a brother, but I've certainly never looked at him like this, either. We have all been friends for so many years that he was just a piece of the puzzle that outlined the last two decades of my life.

I was so in love with Jace that I couldn't see anyone else.

The wind screamed at me from outside the bedroom window.

Leave it to the universe to send me a fuckin' winter storm right when I feel like I'm on the brink of hell.

Tears burned in my eyes, and I did my best to blink them back. Failing miserably, the sniffles started, my body trembling slightly as drops of betrayal slid down my cheeks.

"I know it's little to no consolation seeing as how your mind had taken you somewhere dark, but just so you know, I'm writing to the National Weather Service in Columbia to request that they name a tornado after you."

Bro. What?

Confused, I turned to face him.

"The gawk gawk 8000 you just gave me. That's the kinda shit that will have a man payin' alimony."

I cackled.

"I'm completely serious. I can just see the tornadic resemblance now. First, you suck and blow and then I lose my damn house."

"Oh, my lawd!" I laughed so hard the sound reverberated off the walls. "I guess one of us should send Jace a thank you card – either me for the experience or you for the result."

He giggled.

The room fell abruptly silent, and I could feel the tears start to threaten once again.

"Come here, Loo." He pulled me into his arms, cradling me like the little spoon. "It's gonna get worse before it gets easier, Sugar, but at least we can ping pong between emotionally fucked and emotionally numb together."

I let my neck relax, my tear-stained cheek resting comfortably on his bicep. "Are you going to forgive her?"

I felt him tense behind me.

"Yes. Not because she deserves forgiveness but because I deserve peace."

I nodded against his arm.

"I'm not stayin' with her, though."

I looked back at him over the top of my shoulder.

"If it had just been a one-time thing and she had only hurt me, I might have been able to…," he trailed off. "This wasn't a slip, though. They knowingly and willingly hurt both of us."

A fresh round of tears cascaded down my cheeks.

"That took it from a slip to a character issue." He spoke firmly.

A character issue…

After what seemed like forever, I gathered the courage to say what I had been thinking all day, but unable to admit out loud.

"She asked me this morning if I was sure."

Using his free arm, he rolled me onto my back.

"Sure about what?" He asked, his eyes burning into mine.

"About marrying him. I told her I was and then asked why she would ask me that."

"What was her response?"

"She said she was curious because she knows that the idea of never being with anyone else can be scary. I told her one of the perks of being high school sweethearts was that we would never have to worry about first time jitters again."

He ran his fingers through his short curls before letting his hand come to rest on my stomach.

I continued. "She asked if I felt like I had missed out on anything by never being with anyone else," I recalled. "I asked if she felt that way about you."

He arched an eyebrow.

"She said she was completely satisfied and that she wouldn't change a thing."

He wrinkled his nose in disgust. "The moment when you realize that she wasn't asking because she was being a good friend that wanted to be positive you were sure about marrying him; she was asking because she was hoping you would say you weren't."

Thanks for that incredibly obvious insight, pal.

"And if that moment of realization wasn't enough to gut you, throw in the full-fledged fuckin' clarity that she didn't mean she was completely satisfied with me. She meant she was completely satisfied with fuckin' him."

And said she wouldn't change a thing.

Dakota

This new information had my head spinning.

The depth of deceit is bad enough but the audacity to know you're boning your childhood best friend's man and say you wouldn't change a thing…

Lena burrowed a little deeper against my chest, the small movement sending a whiff of shampoo and vanilla out into the atmosphere.

"Your hair smells good."

Reflexively, she reached out and touched her scalp.

"Ain't no way. Blaine wouldn't let me wash it this morning," she complained.

She sounded so annoyed that I couldn't help but laugh. "Well, he is the expert."

She agreed with a nod. "He said the hair would hold better if it had some natural oil in it. I guess he was right because all hell may have broken loose, but them curls are still intact."

I studied her using the light from the fireplace. She was right and so was Blaine. Her blonde, perfectly round curls covered my arm and a part of both of our pillows.

"For what it's worth, you looked beautiful today," I heard myself say.

Well, she did...

She didn't respond but I could feel her smile against my chest. I pulled her closer.

This is quite literally the last thing we should be doing.

Even with the mental acknowledgement that I shouldn't be holding her this close, or even holding her at all, every part of me wanted to hold her even closer.

Not sure she could get any closer, bud, without you being inside her.

My dick lurched at the mere thought, the subtle twitch pushing against her thigh.

"Felt that," she called out.

Well, you could have acted like you didn't because now it knows you know.

"I have no idea what you're talkin' about," I lied.

"Uh huh." She pressed her thigh against my groin.

Immediately, I tensed, which only made me harder.

"Aight, now," I warned.

She giggled. "Hey Dak?"

Hey?

"Ma'am?"

"What are we gonna do tomorrow?"

Do you want specifics or...?

"Same thing we did today. Deal with it as best we can. Oh, and drink. Definitely drink."

She sighed. "I just feel like once the sun comes up, we will be forced to accept that this is our reality," she admitted.

"Honey, we probably won't see the sun for a few days because of the storm but this is our reality whether it comes up or not."

"Can't we just...reject it?"

Reality?

"Nah, but we can learn from it."

Jolene

A subtle light flooded the room.

Guess we survived the night.

I was still curled up next to Dakota, his strong, tattooed arms holding me firmly against his chest.

How do I free myself without waking him?

I tried inching my way out of his grasp, but he only gripped me tighter. I wriggled a little hoping he would take the hint and release me. His eyes flew open and then widened in surprise.

You were expecting a slutty, hot brunette, huh?

"Lena." He loosened his hold.

"Yeah… good morning." I slid back to my side of the bed.

"Mornin'," he responded, rubbing his slight five o'clock shadow.

"Still no power," I pointed out lamely.

"I see that."

Of course he sees it, Lena. Not to mention, it's fuckin' freezing in here.

We lay there in silence.

"I'm gonna try to go into town and grab some groceries," he announced. "The roads are likely already too shitty to drive back to Creek's Edge – not that we wanted to anyways – but my truck can probably make it to town."

"Can I go?" I asked quietly.

He nodded. "We need to grab your bag so you can get something warm to wear that doesn't swallow you, though. I'll go get it."

I smiled. "Thanks, pal."

I watched as he climbed out of bed. He was doing his best to conceal the fact that every part of him knew that it was morning.

Giggling, I shook my head.

Pain radiated from one temple to the other.

That would be a direct consequence of Jack Daniels and a jackass.

I dragged myself out of bed, already dreading going downstairs where the temperature would definitely be much cooler. Our fire, even now at barely a smolder, had kept the room at somewhat of a comfortable temperature throughout the night.

It wasn't the fire. It was the 6'4" firefighter that's built sturdier than a brick shithouse.

I made my way downstairs, the frigid air slicing right through my borrowed, threadbare t-shirt. No sooner than I hit the bottom step, Dakota walked in the front door.

"It's fuckin' freezing and I had to walk over the river, through the woods, and clean past Grandmama's house to get to your damn car!"

I laughed so hard I snorted.

"I'm glad it's funny. Get dressed." He sat my bag down.

Rolling my eyes, I picked it up. "Cool your nuts. I'm goin'."

"My nuts froze and fell off somewhere between the front porch and where you parked your car in bum fuck Egypt."

Giggling, I closed the bathroom door.

Please tell me I packed something warm.

Technically, this was supposed to be my honeymoon, and I had planned on being naked for most of it. Thankfully, I had packed my thick sweatpants and my favorite Georgia Bulldogs hoodie. After dressing in record time, I glanced at myself in the mirror to survey the damage.

You actually don't look half bad, girlfriend. You'd never know that your life fell the fuck apart yesterday.

Opening the bathroom door, I hollered his name.

He stepped out from behind the wall. "I'm right here. Why are you carryin' on with all that hollerin'?"

"Because I can," I grinned. "Let's go."

107

Dakota

The drive into town was easier than I expected.

Maybe the storm side swiped us.

I turned in the parking lot of Mr. Paul's General Store, my truck bouncing over a pothole in the old gravel.

"Jeez!" Lena exclaimed, dramatically grabbing the Oh Shit Handle.

I rolled my eyes. "Damn, you almost overreacted to something."

Laughing, she let go of the handle. "Maybe the storm skipped us," she remarked. "There's nobody here."

"I was thinkin' that on the way here when I saw how normal the roads seem."

We climbed out in unison and headed for the door. I opened it and held it, gesturing for her to go on inside. "Demons, first."

Another hearty laugh.

Why is that sound like a fuckin' drug for me today?

"Lena! Dakota!" a familiar voice called out.

Mrs. Rosie, the owner's wife, barreled at us from behind the wooden counter. She embraced Lena first, hugging her neck tightly before releasing her to do the same to me.

"It's been a minute!" She looked behind us. "Where's Jace and Cassie?"

Lena and I exchanged glances.

"That's a good question," Lena responded.

Mrs. Rosie shot me a worried glance. She and Mr. Paul have known me since I was a little boy. They bought the general store when I was about two years old, renovating and reopening it for all the locals. Since it's the only store in town, I'd been in here a few thousand times over the last thirty years.

"Oh, dear. I hope everything is alright!" Her voice was full of concern.

"It is!" Lena responded a little too cheerfully.

We came to get some groceries for the house because of the winter storm warning but it seems like it may have passed right by us," I explained, glancing out the front door.

Mrs. Rosie looked at me like I'd lost my mind. "Dollbaby, those new, fancy phones y'all kids tote around don't tell you 'bout the weather? It hasn't even hit us yet!"

"My phone is dead, and I forgot my charger," I fibbed.

She nodded. "I gotcha. Well, we have some chargers back there and we are pretty well stocked – food wise – but we are clean out of flashlights and candles. Apparently, the wind knocked down a tree on the north side of the mountain last night and caused some power outages."

"Belleview was one of them," Lena explained. "I can do the dark, but I don't do hungry!"

Mrs. Rosie gave us a warm chuckle. "You kids grab a buggy and go find what you need. If you need me, I'll be watching my programs."

"Yes, ma'am, thank you!"

I love that woman.

Lena and I walked towards the other side of the building.

"Her programs," she mused. "You think she's a Young and the Restless girlie or an All My Children fanatic?"

"Definitely, Young and the Restless." I thought back to my childhood, remembering the unmistakable sound of the Y&R theme song playing when Dad would bring me in for a bag of candy.

"Can't blame her. Victor Newman could scramble my eggs."

The laugh that got out of me was so deep that it felt like it came from my ankles.

"You're insane," I told her. "Seriously. A fuckin' loon."

She grinned at me as she tossed a package of cookies into the buggy.

This shopping trip is going to be like someone turned a bunch of twelve-year-olds loose and told them to pick their favorite things.

An hour later, we were standing at the counter, a couple weeks' worth of food gliding up the conveyor belt.

How long are we planning to hide out up here?

As Mrs. Rosie finished ringing everything up, Lena pulled her card from the pocket of her sweatpants. Quicker than a ninja, I snatched it out of her hand.

"Yeah, right," I told her as I pulled out my wallet and passed Mrs. Rosie my card.

Lena rolled her eyes. "I picked out most of that so let me pay for it!"

"Yeah, no. I'm paying."

From across the counter, Mrs. Rosie smiled. "You forgot a charger!" She reminded me before hurrying away from the register. She returned a moment later with an electric orange cord. "This one works for all the phones!"

All the phones...

"Thank you for remembering!"

I finished paying and we said our goodbyes, but not before Mrs. Rosie made us promise to come back while we were here so Mr. Paul could see us.

The air was even colder when we stepped out the front door. Fetching my keys from my pocket, I pressed my remote start button.

"Get in, Loo. I'll load up."

Surprisingly, she obeyed my request.

Only because she doesn't like the cold.

Five minutes later, everything was loaded in the bed of my truck except for the phone charger I really didn't need for a phone that I really didn't give a fuck to turn on.

Jolene

"Do y'all have a weather radio?"

He turned to me, confused.

"Probably. Why?"

I sighed. "I just don't want to cut my damn phone back on to stay updated on the weather, but we probably should stay updated on what's going on," I explained.

"We probably have one in a closet somewhere, but even if we don't, we can call your parents and my dad from the house phone to let them know we're okay and then just ride out the storm. We are prepared, I think."

You think?

"Do house phones work if there's no power?"

He bit his lip. "Ya know, I'm not sure. Either way, we will update the people who deserve updates and fuck the rest. I'm goin' to make sure there's plenty of firewood when we get back. We can either cook something on the grill for supper tonight or eat some of the Chef Boyardee crap you picked out at Paul's."

I nodded and turned to stare out the window. I have always loved riding to the mountain house but even the view couldn't lift my spirits today.

Dakota reached over the console and patted my thigh. "I've got you, Lena."

I squeezed his hand appreciatively. As I went to pull away, he held on, encircling my fingers with his own as if they were meant to be mixed up together.

We drove back to the cabin in silence, our hands meshed and resting on my thigh. Every now and then, he would rub the top of my knuckles with his thumb.

He pulled up to the front porch. "Go inside and start a fire in the living room, Boy Scout. I'll bring our survival shit inside."

Laughing, I climbed out of his truck.

The air inside the cabin was sharp and cold. Kneeling at the fireplace, I rearranged the logs to make sure the oxygen would be able to get through them. As I admired my handy work, Dak dropped two armloads of groceries on the kitchen countertop.

"Dispatch, be advised, there's no flames showing," he teased.

Dispatch, be advised I'm about to smack your lieutenant.

"I'm tryin', bitch! I was rearranging everything so the oxygen could feed the logs!"

He looked up from unloading the grocery bags, clearly impressed by what I had said.

I was with y'all all through the fire academy and I've spent the last twelve years listening to y'all talk about it.

I struck a match across the brick, tossed it in the enormous opening, and watched the fire roar to life.

"Good girl."

My pulse quickened.

Why have you said that about fifteen times in the last twelve hours?

"I hope you're not seriously impressed that I can build a fire" I giggled.

"I'm impressed that you have the initiative," he explained as he put the groceries away.

Is that a compliment?

"I'll get all that put up. You go make sure we have wood!"

"Yes, ma'am," he responded, abandoning a pack of steaks near the stove.

Do I ever put the cold stuff in the fridge or just sit it out on the damn porch? Fuckin' power outage.

Gathering all the perishables, I hauled them out to the back deck. From somewhere in the yard, I could hear Dakota's voice.

Who the fuck is he talking to? Sir, this is the wilderness.

I began pulling things out of the brown paper sacks, sitting them out neatly on the old picnic table. Off in the distance, I heard Dakota laugh.

What the fuck?

I opened a carton of eggs so the cold air could get to them.

One thing all southerners will tell you is that we prefer a winter power outage to one in the summertime. If the power goes out this time of year, we just stick our groceries out on a table in the yard, fully confident that that outdoor temperatures will keep things from spoiling.

As I finished unloading all the things, Dak's laugh echoed through the trees.

Someone is gettin' real close to needin' a grippy sock vacation.

Dakota

"Lena?"

No answer.

"Lena Loo!"

Still nothing.

"Jolene! Where you at?" My voice ricocheted off the cabin walls.

Where the hell did she go?

I took the stairs two at a time, silently thanking the Lord for keeping me from breaking my neck.

This house is so damn dark.

I found her upstairs, sound asleep across her bed. She was laying on her stomach with her feet dangling off, her long hair partially covering her face. As quietly as I could, I pulled my Great Grandmama's quilt off the rocker, draping it across her gently.

Wanting to make sure she was as comfortable as possible, I grabbed a few pieces of wood from the rack, setting them up neatly inside the fireplace.

Where did I put the matches?

I spied them sitting up on the dresser.

I better strike it on the brick, so she doesn't come up from a sound sleep to tell me I'm doing it wrong.

The idea made me smile.

Her way worked like a charm, the jagged brick igniting the match flame at once.

I built her a healthy fire, guaranteed to keep her and the room warm.

I'll keep checking on it to make sure it doesn't go out.

Back downstairs, I set out to find a weather radio, some flashlights and some candles.

I didn't take me long to find the radio but that's where my luck ran out.

How are there no flashlights or candles of any kind mixed in with hundreds of years' worth of shit?

Frustrated, I poured myself a glass of Jack Daniels.

We have plenty of wood, a fuck ton of food, and a perfect view of the mountains. We'll be okay.

"I cannot believe this is my fuckin' life," I muttered softly to myself. "The insane part is that it's all real."

I took another sip of my whiskey.

I might better head to the liquor store before this shit starts.

I put the glass down. Two decent swallows were nowhere near the level it would take to impair my driving, but I was never the type to take the risk. As I waited for those sips to leave my system, I busied myself with bringing more wood up on the back deck.

Jolene

Where the fuck is he?

As I looked around the yard, I felt my pulse quicken.

"Dakota!" My voice rippled through the trees.

I was starting to panic. I never meant to fall asleep when I went upstairs, but when I woke up and came down, he was gone.

"You should have stayed on the deck and kept an eye on him, Lena," I lectured myself.

Now, he's probably gone and gotten himself eaten by a bear.

"Fuck!" I shouted. "I'm scarin' my fuckin' self!"

I climbed the stairs on the back deck.

Maybe he is inside. He could have come through the front door.

I slid the door open. "Dak?"

Nothing.

Maybe he went back to Creek's Edge.

Suddenly, the front door swung open, and he appeared, two big paper bags in his arms.

"Dakota! What the fuck!" Without warning, I burst into tears. In an instant, he was at my side, the bags tossed over the back of the couch.

"What's wrong?" He asked, alarmed, but my words decided not to work.

Speak, bitch.

"What happened, Lena?" He asked again, pulling me into his arms. Still unable to speak, I sobbed into his shoulder.

Maybe I'm the one that needs a grippy sock vacation.

"Shhh…" He soothed me, his hand smoothing down my hair. "Tell me what happened," he demanded gently.

Finally, I found my voice. "I thought something happened to you! I thought you had gone home or fell down the mountain or a bear had eaten you or…" I trailed off.

"A bear?" He asked, his eyes twinkling with amusement. "No, I didn't become bear chow."

I smacked his chest. "It's not funny, fuck face! I was genuinely worried."

Kissing the top of my head, he released me. "I'm sorry I worried you. Mr. Driggers from up the road stopped by when I was out there messin' with the wood. He said that now the news is saying we could get around two feet of snow and ice, so I decided to go to the liquor store before it got bad."

It didn't even occur to me to check the yard for his truck.

"Two feet? Holy shit."

"Yeah, I know. The liquor store had one flashlight left and some batteries but no candles. I grabbed the light and the batteries because I found a weather radio."

I nodded. "Okay."

"I think between the fire light and the flashlight, we will make do. I can't believe we didn't have any candles in this damn place," he remarked. "Now, we know we need to stock this place back up before next winter."

"I have some candles in my car."

He eyed me curiously. "Orders you haven't dropped off?"

Uhhh, no. That's just bad business.

"No. I packed some to set the mood for…" I trailed off. "Anyway, I have some."

"Awesome sauce. Where are they at in your car? If I start the trek now to get them, I might be back by nightfall."

I rolled my eyes. "In the back. They're in a bag with my initials."

He laughed. "That ought to narrow it down."

As he walked his sarcastic ass out the front door, I peeked into the discarded bags he left on the couch.

Three bottles of Jack Daniels, a bottle of Patron, a bottle of vodka, a flashlight, some batteries, and a bottle of orange juice.

Damn, so it's that kinda party.

Dakota

"Some candles, my ass," I muttered to myself as I carried the big ass bag up the front steps. Sitting the haul down, I opened the front door. Lena was unpacking the liquor, setting it up neatly on the bar shelf.

"You must have wiped out all of your inventory prepping for your honeymoon."

Turning around, she shot me a glare. "There's only about fifteen candles in there."

Fifteen heavy ass candles.

Reaching inside the bag, I pulled out a jar that was on top. It was a pink candle labeled *"Company's Comin'"*.

"What does this one smell like?" I inquired.

"Clean laundry. I'm thinkin' about changing up my label to include a scent description."

Removing the lid, I raised the jar to my nose.

Damn, that really does smell like fabric softener.

Replacing the lid, I examined the label.

It was simple – white with *Creek's Edge Candle Co.* at the top and the name of the candle just beneath it in a minimalist font.

Simple and to the point.

"I think it's great like it is." I sat the jar on the countertop.

She smiled. "Yeah?" I nodded.

"Yep, some things just don't need extra fuss. The incredibility speaks for itself."

"Maybe not, but some folks might like knowing exactly what they're gettin' ahead of time," she pointed out.

"If you like it how it is, don't change it up to appease someone else."

The warm look she gave me told me she knew I wasn't talking about the candles.

Placing the last bottle of alcohol on the shelf, she turned to me. "Okay, roomie. What are you grillin' for supper?"

Jolene

"That was delicious," I told Dakota after polishing off my last bite of steak. "It was cooked perfectly."

He smiled. "I'm glad you enjoyed it."

The fire roared in front of us.

"I did. Sounds like you finished just in time, too." I pointed at the ceiling.

Frozen rain pelted the tin roof, a sound guaranteed to lull you to sleep if you focused on it long enough.

He grabbed my plate and carried it to the sink.

How are we gonna wash those?

Grabbing a familiar bottle, he poured himself another glass of whiskey. "Need another?" He asked.

Nodding, I raised my glass. "You win the best bartender award."

"I'm the only bartender," he pointed out, filling my solo cup to the brim.

"I didn't say you had a lot of competition. I said you were the best."

Sitting the bottle on the coffee table, he rolled his eyes. "I'll carry the title proudly."

"As you should."

We stared at the fire in silence, the flames making the shadows dance.

"We forgot to call our parents!" I jumped up. "Fuck!"

The room wiggled a little, either from the Jack or the jumping up so quickly.

"Relax." He took another sip. "I called Big Jake, Chief Hennessy, and your parents earlier on the way to the liquor store."

What?

"You were callin' everybody in Creek's Edge, and you couldn't call me to tell me where you were so I would know that you weren't dead?"

"Your phone was off, fruit loop," he reminded me. "I sent a text, but it didn't deliver."

Oh yeah... I'm ridiculous.

"I forgot. What did my parents say?"

He chuckled. "They were grateful you weren't up here alone. Your daddy thanked me for clockin' Jace."

Sounds like daddy.

"It's a wonder he didn't get him before you did. You know my daddy don't play 'bout me."

He laughed. "I think the only thing that stopped him was your mama. The only thing he is more adamant about than protecting you is listenin' to Mrs. Charlie."

I smiled proudly. "You ain't wrong. He does his best not to ruffle her feathers."

"All men should take notes."

Using the hair tie on my wrist, I twisted my hair into a neat bun. "Mutual respect is all I'm after. Oh, and not stickin' your dick in my friends."

"What a coincidence. I like my coffee a little similar. Without other people's dick in it."

The sip of whiskey I was trying to swallow came flying out of my nose and I started to sputter.

He reached over, patting me on the back. "You okay? What the fuck was that?"

"I was tryin' to swallow, and you made me laugh… now I'm sticky!" I whined.

"So many jokes, so little time."

I rolled my eyes. "Shut up. I'm sticky now and I can't shower!"

I hate being unable to shower.

"Go get in the hot tub," he suggested. "I'll go with you."

In a winter storm, bro?

"It's literally sleeting outside," I reminded him.

He stood up, extending his arm to help me to my feet. "So? The back deck is covered, and the water is hot. It's in the description."

Fair point even if the execution was smartassed as fuck.

He waved his arm impatiently, encouraging me to grab it. I took it and he yanked me to my feet.

"I didn't bring a bathing suit.," I explained. "I figured if we were goin' to get in the hot tub, we would just –" He held his hand up.

"Eww, please stop. Just go in your underwear."

Yeah, because that's smart.

"It's the same as a bikini, Jolene." He spoke, his voice stained with exasperation.

He's so fun to annoy.

"Okay, but I'm wearing a tank top and not a bra. My bras are expensive as fuck and that chlorine might fuck them up." I peeled off my hoodie, my skin pebbling as the cool, cabin air hit my bare skin.

He looked shocked, clearly expecting me to go into the bathroom to change.

I have on a tank top and panties already. Going into the bathroom and coming out half naked would be weird.

Shrugging, he hooked his fingers in his waistband, sliding his sweats down his toned thighs.

No boner…

A tinge of disappointment hit me square in the chest.

You're a slut, Lena.

"Don't look so sad, it's chilly in here." He smirked.

Am I that fuckin' transparent?

Blushing, I rolled my eyes. "I have no idea what you're talkin' about," I lied.

"Sure, you don't. Take your pants off."

His tone forced a shiver down my spine.

"Yes, daddy," I retorted sarcastically.

"Good girl." He took off towards the back door, sliding the glass open dramatically. "Fuck me sideways! It's cold!"
Coming up behind him, I giggled. "Yeah, that's usually one of the top three indicators of a winter storm."

"I feel like I've said it before but it's worth repeating… you're much more fun to listen to with something in your mouth." He climbed in the hot tub.

Nothing witty came to mind so I stayed silent as I climbed the sidestep to join him.

"Wait!" He hollered. I stopped mid-way through my leg swing. "What?"

It's fuckin' cold, bro.

He pointed at my hips. "Are those the normal folk's kind or are they gonna vanish the second they get wet?"

I looked down at my white cotton briefs. "These are normal."

Accepting that answer, he scooted over, giving me room to climb in and sit down. The water felt incredible in contrast to the freezing air. Closing my eyes, I savored the feeling.

"Fuck!" My eyes flew open, his sudden use of expletives ruining my peaceful moment. "What, bro?"

"We left the whiskey inside!" He waded to the side closest to the door. "And towels!" He climbed over the side with expert balance.

We get it, you're a firefighter.

He returned a moment later with the bottle of Jack Daniels and two fluffy towels. Grinning, he held up the bottle. "Let's play Never Have I Ever!"

Dakota

"Never have I ever gotten a speeding ticket," she proclaimed proudly. I turned up the bottle.

"That's only because you're pretty. You drive like a bat outta hell."

She laughed. "Your turn."

"Never have I ever been bitten by a dog." She thought it over for a second before reaching for the bottle.

"Never have I ever been inside a burning building."

Cheap shot.

She handed me the bottle. I gulped it quickly before sitting it on the side of the tub.

"Oh, so we playin' like that?"

She laughed.

"Okay, princess, never have I ever made a candle." She grabbed the bottle and turned it up.

"Never have I ever saved someone's life."

Another sip for me. *And proud of that one.*

"Never have I ever painted my nails."

Another sip for her.

We may as well just drink without the game…

I should have pointed it out, but I didn't. I was having too much fun playing Battle Shots with her.

"Never have I ever worn an oxygen tank."

Another for me.

"Never have I ever curled my hair."

"Oh, you're just graspin' at straws now." She stood and snatched the bottle, the movement revealing her extremely transparent tank top. My dick grew underneath the water.

Should I point out that her shirt is see through?

She passed me the bottle. "Why are you makin' that face?" she asked.

You're too respectful not to let her know.

"Your shirt is see through."

She looked down immediately and shrugged. "Well, you saw them last night anyways, right?"

"Yeah…"

"Okay then, I didn't think about the fact that it would be see through, but all I brought with me are white tank tops."

I've never seen her in anything white before this weekend. It's always black.

"I know, I always wear black," she spoke, reading my mind. "I was tryin' to be all bridal and shit." She looked so sad at her own explanation.

"Hey, it's okay." I reached out for her. She shook her head. "I'm okay. I also just remembered that my panties are white and probably fuckin' see through, too."

Why do I want to see?

"Stand up and let's see."

You were supposed to think it, not say it!

Obediently, she stood on the ledge of the hot tub.

Okay, that's enough Jack Daniels for tonight.

"Are they see through?"

I looked at her closely. Her panties looked like melting sugar, the fabric barely glazing her swollen, bare pussy.

Goddamn!

"Yes."

"I figured." She reached down and touched herself, the contact hardening her clit immediately.

Please, sit the fuck down.

"I don't know why you're makin' a disgusted face like every bit of this wasn't in your mouth last night," she snapped, sitting down with an abrupt splash.

The fuck?

"What?"

"Nothing. Give me the bottle."

Absolutely the fuck not.

I moved the bottle out of her reach. "You think I'm disgusted?"

She didn't say a word.

"Lena."

She only nodded.

You gon' learn today.

Reaching under the water, I grabbed her by her hips, lifting her to the side of the tub. Shrieking in surprise, she grabbed my head to keep from falling over the side.

I spread her legs. "You think seein' this bothered me?"

She was too stunned to speak.

"You think this…" I brushed my thumb against her swollen lips. "…bothered me?" I grazed her with my thumb again, her body jolting at the contact.

Okay, I'm gonna need you to say something.

"Lena."

"I don't know…the look on your face…" she trailed off.

I took my hands off her, my dick protesting immediately.

She's unsure and we aren't doing it under those circumstances.

"Why did you stop?"

"You didn't seem comfortable and making sure you are - that is my number one focus."

"I'm just cold. Warm me up."

Or just get back in the water so we can both start thinkin' clearly.

"Climb back down into the water," I instructed, reaching for her hand. Taking my hand, she placed it against her pussy.

"Make me forget that I'm cold."

Abort mission. Abort mission.

I rubbed her through the wet cotton. The sound she made was louder than the sleet on the tin roof.

I tapped on her clit. She yelped and jumped, lifting her hips in search of anything to get her to her release. I stroked her with my thumb, my eyes fixated on her tits bouncing inside her sodden shirt.

"Please, keep doin' it just like that," she pleaded. "I'm gettin' so close."

Increasing the pressure, I pinched her throbbing clit, rolling it between my thumb and index finger. She erupted, her body convulsing as her orgasm drove through her.

"Fuckkkk, I'm cumming!"

Do it quietly before I wind up fuckin' you over the side of this hot tub.

"Cum again, baby," I ordered, rubbing her harder, faster. "Cum again, Lena. Now."

Leaning over, I sucked her clit through the fabric, reaching up to play with her nipples as I sucked. She screamed, her body quaking as wave after wave of intensity shattered her. Finally, I pulled away, satisfied that I'd warmed her up.

"Dak, that was –"

"Lena!" A deep voice interrupted.

Fuckin' Jace.

Jolene

"Lena!" Jace's voice bellowed from inside the dimly lit cabin.

What the fuck?

Dakota stood up in the water, the boner that he hopefully had a moment ago, long gone. "The fuck is he doin' here?" He demanded angrily.

"I'll give you one guess."

Climbing out, he wrapped a towel around his waist before holding the remaining towel out to me.

"C'mon, I'll handle this shit right now," he promised. "Starting with getting' that motherfucker out of my goddamn house."

Standing on the ledge, I wrapped the warm towel around myself, praying for my legs to do what legs are supposed to do.

Is my adrenaline pumping this hard or is this from the alcohol?

Taking his outstretched hand, I stepped down onto the deck. He flung back the sliding door and stepped inside; his hand still entangled with mine. Before we could make it to the sofa, Jace appeared at the bottom of the staircase, my former friend coming down the stairs behind him.

Oh joy.

I tried pulling my hand away, but Dak only tightened his grip.

That's not gonna help anything, Dakota.

"What the fuck are y'all doin' here?" he demanded, his voice dripping venom.

Jace, whose black eye and busted lip was obvious even in the dimly lit living room, ignored him, turning his attention only to me. "Lena, can we please go upstairs and talk?"

"No." It was a complete sentence.

"Lena, come on." He took a step towards me, an innocent gesture that looked menacing by firelight. Dakota moved in between us, twisting his arm behind him so he didn't have to let go of my hand.

"I'm goin' to talk to my fiancé," Jace informed him.

"I don't give a fuck about your history with her. If you so much as glance in her direction again, the place I take you will make hell seem like a happy place."

Behind Jace, Cassie stood with widened eyes. "Dak," she purred. "Let them talk so we can talk."

Dakota laughed. "I don't give a damn about anything you have to say. Y'all get the hell outta my house. The door is right where you left it." He pulled me to his side.

Jace's eyes burned with anger. "We aren't leaving. The roads are iced over."

"Should have thought of that before you drove your dumbasses up here," Dak responded nonchalantly.

With my free hand, I touched Dak's dripping shoulder. "Let them stay. We don't want to be the reason a first responder has to get out in this weather to pull these idiots out of a ditch," I reasoned.

Dak thought it over. "Good point, Lena Loo. Y'all can sleep down here. Firewood is in the rack."

He finally released my hand before walking over to the kitchen island. "There it is!" He spoke to no one in particular as he bent to grab my bag of candles.

Breezing back over to me, he grabbed my hand and led me up the stairs, brushing past Jace as if he wasn't standing there. Cassie stood there open mouthed, clearly stunned by the scene unfolding in front of her. She reached out to touch him but failed, thanks to the wideness of the dark stairway.

"Don't touch me, Cassie." His voice was lethal.

At the top of the stairs, he barreled into the master bedroom, banging the bag of candles on the doorframe as he entered.

Uhhh, that's my room.

I followed him into the large space, shutting the door behind me.

"You cannot sleep in here," I informed him. "They're downstairs."

"Fuckin' watch me."

He used the flashlight he stashed up here before supper to find the matches. He lifted the bag of candles onto the bed, reaching in and grabbing two in one hand. Walking over to the fireplace, he dragged the match across the brick, using the spark he created to light the candles.

"I know you're smirking," he told me. "Yes, the brick is effective"

I know it.

He placed the lit candles on top of the dresser before grabbing two more from the bag. Repeating my brick method, he added two more sources of light to the room.

"Now, the fire"

The mention of the fire reminded me that I was wearing clothes that were soaking wet and a towel that was headed in the same direction. Dak was crouched down at the fireplace, my soggy towel's twin around his waist.

"Uhhh, Dak?"

"Hmmm?" He continued grabbing wood from the rack, never bothering to look up.

"Dakota." He looked up immediately that time, likely because of the tone of my voice.

"Our clothes are downstairs."

"Okay?" He looked confused.

"Our. Clothes. Are. Downstairs." I repeated, emphatically.

Realization flashed across his face. "Oh well."

What the fuck you mean "oh well"?

"What do you mean 'oh well'… I'm cold!"

As if by magic, the fire came to life, the glow basking the entire room in burnt orange.

"I know you're cold. I built you a fire." He pointed proudly at the flickering flames.

"Which I appreciate, but I still have no dry clothes up here so I'm going to grab our bags."

I was only able to take one step towards the door before he grabbed my arm.

"Open that door and I'm tyin' you to the bed."

I'm sorry, what?

"Bitch, I'm cold!" I protested. "We need something dry, or we are gonna catch pneumonia!"

"You heard me, Lena, but go ahead and try me if you want to."

His threat sounded delicious.

"So, what the fuck do you expect me to do?" I demanded.

"Take off your wet clothes."

And put on what, my guy?

"I have nothin' else to put on! What part of that is unclear?!"

"So, be naked! I've made you cum twice in the last twenty-four hours and I've seen you naked so what difference could it possibly make?"

I blushed, but deep down, I knew he had a point. Shrugging my shoulders, I dropped the towel and peeled off my wet clothes.

Dakota

Lena stood before me as naked as the day she was born.

Look at something... anything else... because you're about to have to strip, too, and your thoughts are going to be standing at attention.

"Get into bed and get warm," I ordered.

"The sheets are cold, Dakota!" She fussed. "I'm cold, dammnit!"

Oh, for fuck's sake...

"Oh, my lord, hang on." I unwrapped the towel and yanked down my saturated boxers. "Come here."

"What?"

"Come here. Body heat."

The fire ripped and roared.

"My lord, I'll just get in the cold ass sheets," she grumbled.

"Look at that, you do listen. Thank you."

She stuck her middle finger up at me before climbing under the worn sheets. I added another log to the fire.

"Better?" I asked her.

"Yeah, sure." Her teeth chattered.

Okay, body heat, it is.

Grabbing the old quilt, I draped it across her before climbing into bed beside her.

"We will warm up faster with body heat but if you're not comfortable with that idea, wrap that quilt around you tightly until the fire heats the room up."

She shivered. "Is it too late to choose body heat?"

I pulled her cold, naked body into mine, mentally pleading with my body to act right.

Mamaw…church…that skin graph I had to have that one time…

She hiccupped loudly, her body vibrating against mine.

The Golden Girls… picture it, Sicily 1912… Rose, tell me about St. Olaf…

She hiccupped again.

Ok, get your shit under control, girlie pop.

"Are you alright?"

She giggled. "I have the hiccups!"

Yeah, I caught that…

"Need some Jack?"

Water would probably be better, but ya know…

"Please!"

"Be right back." Releasing her, I climbed out of bed, snagging a candle to guide me before hauling my naked ass down the stairs.

"Dak! Can we please… why are you naked?" Cassie asked, unable to hide the horror in her voice. Jace, who was pacing near the fireplace when I hit the bottom step, stalked towards me, his eyes filled with daggers.

"Make my day, Reynolds."

He stopped dead in his tracks.

Grabbing the bottle of whiskey, I took off up the stairs, giving them the perfect view of the part of me that they could line up to kiss.

Back in the bedroom, I locked the door behind me.

Maybe she got rid of them.

Hiccup.

Or not.

"Did you get something to drink?" she asked, rolling over to face me. I held up the bottle.

"Yes ma'am."

She sat up in bed just enough to give me a good view of her bare chest.

Climbing in next to her, I removed the cap before passing her the bottle. She turned it up for a few seconds, the bubbles scattering as she chugged.

"Thanks, homie." She passed the bottle back to me. Capping it, I put on the nightstand.

Silence stretched between us.

Do I reach over and grab her or see if she says she's cold again?

"Hey Dak?"

"Hmm?"

"Why didn't you grab our bags while you were down there?"

Why didn't I?

"Honestly, I didn't even think about it," I answered truthfully.

"Okay." A shiver shook the bed.

"Body heat?" I asked her.

She nodded just as another hiccup escaped. Scooting up behind her, I pulled her close.

"Is that better?"

She gave a little wiggle.

Girl, lay your ass still.

"Yes, are you comfortable?" She asked cheerfully.

I am, actually.

"Yes ma'am, now go to sleep."

"Night, Dak."

"Night, Loo."

I closed my eyes and tried to sleep but my mind wouldn't let me rest.

How the fuck did I end up naked, snuggling my best friend's former fiancé to keep her warm because we wound up potentially snowed in during, what would be, their honeymoon?

"Can't sleep, either?"

How did she know?

"I guess I have too much on my mind," I admitted.

She rolled to face me, her firm tits pressed against my chest and my dick pushing against her thigh.

"Why are they here?" She asked quietly. "And they came together which helps absolutely nothing."

"They've been doin' a lot of shit together, but I don't give a fuck that they're here."

She raised an eyebrow. "You don't?"

I forgot they were here until you mentioned it.

"I have a hot, naked blonde practically on top of me. I haven't given them a second thought."

Mainly because he played the fuck out of himself.

Jolene

His eyes twinkled from the light of the fire.

"The second I saw them; my mind took me right back to walkin' in on them. The sound of it is just replaying in my head, over and over."

He reached out to rub my arm. I felt the tears threatening.

"What can I do to make it better?" He asked gently.

"I don't know. I just want them to hurt – to hurt the way they hurt us."

He nodded. "I know."

I wrapped my arm around his neck, lightly playing with dark curls on the back of his head. Sighing appreciatively, he closed his eyes.

Suddenly feeling bold, I leaned in and pressed my lips against his throat. He growled, a deep animalistic sound that vibrated against my lips.

Should I stop?

He grabbed the back of my head, twisting his fingers in my hair. Damn near paralyzed in fear, I tried pulling away.

"Nuh uh," he grumbled, holding my mouth to his neck. "Do that again."

I wrapped my lips around his throat, dragging my tongue across his soft skin.

How does he taste so good?

I kissed and rubbed my way to his collarbone.

I felt him pulse against my thigh.

Well, I know, at least, one part of him is enjoyin' this.

He slid his hand down my spine, letting it come to rest across my ass. I nipped my way to his earlobe, teasing it with my tongue. He gripped my ass firmly, lining his hardness up perfectly with my wet slit. A moan I couldn't hold back danced on my lips as he grinded my pussy against him.

How can this feel so fuckin' good?

My orgasm was mounting, my torment to his neck and ears abandoned. I couldn't think of anything except the grinding of his dick against my tender lips.

"Dak." I whimpered against his ear. "I'm gonna cum."

He pressed against me harder; the increased pressure was more than enough to push me over the edge.

"I'm cumming!" I managed, his ear against my mouth. "Please, don't stop!"

He didn't stop. He kept going until my body was trembling like a leaf.

How can I still want more?

"Fuck me," I pleaded.

Dakota

What did she just say?

"Lena, I'm not sure –"

"Please, Dak." She pulled me on top of her.

"I don't have a condom," I informed her.

"IUD." Reaching down, she positioned me at her entrance.

Lord, forgive me cause I'm 'bout to fuckin' sin.

I pushed into her slowly, pausing to let her adjust. Or maybe I paused so that I could adjust. Her pussy was so tight that it felt like her walls were caving in.

What in the gorilla grip?

She lifted her hips, coaxing me to move mine. I started to fuck her slowly, doing my best to make this feeling last as long as I could.

She closed her eyes. "Are you gonna fuck me or just fuck around?"

Don't do that, girl. I will have you so dick whipped that you start hiding in the bushes outside my house.

"On your knees, Lena." I pulled out.

She looked surprised.

"Now."

With a smirk, she flipped on her stomach, pausing a second before arching up onto her knees.

She bends like a goddamn question mark.

I thrust into her hard as I could, prying a scream from between her full lips.

"You want to be fucked?" I asked between thrusts. "Is that what you want?"

"Yes!" She moaned breathlessly, pushing her ass back to meet me.

"Be careful what you ask for," I threatened through clenched teeth.

Grabbing a fistful of her hair, I pulled her back to me, her body arched against my chest. As I fucked her dripping pussy, I reached around and grabbed her tit, pinching and pulling at her hardened nipples.

I felt her clenching around me, her body squeezing me like a vice.

"Did I tell you that you could fuckin' cum? I growled in her ear.

"Did I fuckin' ask?"

Okay, I gotta little firecracker on my hands.

I pushed her face down on the bed, gripping her hips for dear life. My balls slapped against her clit with every thrust inside her.

"Damn, Dak, I thought you enjoyed playin' with fire." She giggled. "Fuck me harder."

Oh, she's one of those that like to be thrown through the wall.

Pulling out, I grabbed her waist violently, hauling her to her knees. By the throat I held her, her mouth inches from my glistening cock.

"Taste what I did to you since you wanna be cute." I shoved myself between her lips, pausing only a fraction when I felt my sensitive head hit her tonsils. She gagged but didn't stop, only grabbed my hips to take me deeper.

"Fuck, Lena, you're so damn good with your mouth," I croaked.

She pulled me closer as she bobbed on my cock, digging her wedding nails into my ass cheeks so deep that she had to have drawn blood.

The rubber band on my restraint snapped.

Twisting her hair into a makeshift ponytail, I punished her throat, fucking it as if I'd never get another chance.

You probably won't.

Her eyes watered from the thickness, and she started to choke.

"You're taking me like such a good girl," I managed. "So deep in your fuckin' throat."

She tilted her head back, the angle giving me the best access to her gag reflexes. Hearing her choke was so fucking sexy, it was damn near pushing me over the edge.

I don't want to finish like this.

Hating every goddamn second of it, I withdrew from her mouth. She pouted, her swollen lips fixed in a frown. I grinned and flopped on my back next to her.

"Ride my cock."

My good girl straddled me, guiding me back inside her juicy opening. She buried herself to the hilt, my overly sensitive head pressing against her cervix.

"So deep," she groaned, rolling her hips to accommodate my size. "You're stretching me wide open."

I stayed still, allowing her to adjust without pain. She started bouncing her ass, strategically grinding her clit against my skin. I closed my eyes and let her ride, relishing the feeling of her wrapped around me. Without warning, she stopped.

"I want to turn around."

Without waiting for my acceptance, she spun around on my dick, her ass now resting against my waist. Rubbing her clit furiously, she rocked, and she bounced, the double sensation too much for her body to endure.

"I'm cumming! Fuck! I'm cumming!"

Reaching under her thighs, I lifted her legs, beating up her pussy as if it deserved it. With my arm under her thigh, I held her around her waist, forcing her to take her punishment. I fucked her hard and I fucked her good, her voice echoing my name off the walls. My legs started to tremble, and she knew I was close, her throaty moans nearly taking me all the way.

"Cum on my tongue, Dakota."

Chill out, girl, before I fuckin' propose.

She climbed off in a huff, leaving her juices behind, the evidence too much to ignore.

She gets so fuckin' wet.

Kneeling on the floor in front of the bed, she stared at me with innocent eyes. I struggled to my knees, wobbling, as her small palm latched around my throbbing cock. Deep throating me with ease, she used me to massage her tonsils, gagging as if were her favorite thing to do.

"Lena," I begged. "Please."

I don't know what I was begging her for, I just needed her to fucking do it. Pulling me out of her perfect mouth, she spit on me, using her thick saliva to jack me off. With an evil look in her eyes, she slapped me against her tongue.

"Have I been a good enough girl yet to earn your cum?"

With those words on her lips, I exploded, coating her tongue with my warm, thick cum.

So, this is what someone means when they say that their soul left their body...

Jolene

I have never had a single complaint about the sex life that Jace and I had together… until I realized what I was missing.

I have never been more perfectly or thoroughly fucked.

Dak and I laid together in sweaty naked silence.

"Are you okay?" He asked gently.

Sighing blissfully, I nodded. "I'm okay… are you?"

He laughed. "I have found a new preferred method of cardio. Damn near felt like my heart was gonna explode for a minute or two."

"Definitely more fun than the gym," I agreed. "You stretched me more than any fitness instructor ever has."

Chuckling, he pulled me closer, my head coming to rest on his shoulder.

Abruptly, realization hit me square in the gut.

"You know what I just remembered?" I asked.

"Hmmm?" He stroked my arm.

"They're downstairs and they probably heard us."

He tensed briefly before shrugging his shoulders. "We can invoice them."

What?

"Invoice them?" I was confused.

"Yep, because we likely just taught them a thing or two and education ain't free."

I laughed from my soul, the tiny part that Dakota didn't fuck into oblivion.

"I'm surprised they didn't come busting up in here" I mused.

"Jace is a fuckin' idiot but he doesn't have a death wish," he responded calmly.

His tone made my stomach dip, but his words made my pussy throb.

The fuck around and find out version of Dakota is pretty fucking sexy.

"You're probably right," I agreed.

"Trust me, he knows better. He won't get a second chance to hurt you so long as there's a breath in my body."

Nuzzling into him, I kissed his chest.

"I think we earned a nap, Lena Loo." He stroked my bare back.

"I think so, too."

Because I really want to do all that again when I wake up.

Dakota

The dimmest of morning glow creeped into the room.

Lena was curled up next to me, snoring like a grown ass man.

Girl, you got that sloppy toppy sexpertise and that sleep apnea.

The fire had been reduced to nothing but a thick layer of glowing ashes.

And yet somehow, I'm still snug as a bug in a rug.

On the nightstand, a *Creek's Edge Candle Co.* flickered, reminding me that I was careless last night in more ways than one.

What was more dangerous, fuckin' my best ex's best friend or leaving lit candles burning without supervision?

The thought of Cassie forced me to remember that she and Jace were downstairs. Careful not to wake up Lena, I climbed out of bed. The floor was freezing underneath my bare feet, and the cabin air was chilling to the bone.

At least my boxers should be dry.

Snagging them from the brick hearth, I was relieved to find that they were stiff as a board, but definitely dry. I slid them on quietly, doing my best to not interrupt the sawing of logs that was occurring on the bed. Looking around the room, I realized I had no idea what I was supposed to be doing. There was nothing to do but… nothing.

I need to fix this piss poor excuse of a fire.

Realistically, I knew I needed to clean all the ashes out before I added more wood, but I didn't want her to wake up cold.

Using the fire poker, I broke up the rest of the kindling logs. The ashes flamed up for a moment before returning to a deep glow. I added a few small pieces of wood and fat lighter, bringing the weak, warm glimmer to life. It wouldn't do much before the surrounding ashes suffocated the flow of air, but it would knock a little bit of the chill out of the air.

In the words of the great Major Payne, it's still a shit sandwich, it's just not a soggy one.

Behind me, a sleepy voice spoke up. "Not much for sleepin' in?"

"I didn't want you to wake up cold," I told her. "It was cold in here."

"Well, ain't you sweet?"

I laughed. "Don't tell anyone."

She gave me the scout's honor sign. "I see you found your drawers." I looked down automatically.

"I did. Do you want yours?"

She hesitated for a moment before nodding her head. I tossed her the bra and panties. Standing up in bed, she took her time putting them on.

Well, good mornin'.

"How are you feelin'?" I asked her as I sat down at the foot of the bed.

"I feel incredible!" She pulled the sheet around her.

Why does hearing that make the entire morning better?

'Glad to hear it. You're not sore?"

"Oh, my vag feels like you beat it for insulting your Mamaw's potato salad, but I'm loving it."

I howled with laughter. "You're ridiculous." I tossed the quilt over her head.

Giggling, she pulled it off, turning her long hair into a static mess.

"Did it snow?" she asked.

That's a good question.

"Ya know, I don't know. I haven't checked."

With an eyeroll, she jumped out of bed and darted to the window. She shrieked excitedly, "Dak! Look!"

I joined her at the window. The backyard, covered in a heavy blanket of snow, looked like something out of a snow globe after someone furiously shakes it up. Thick snowflakes swirled through the air, sticking to everything that they landed on. The scenery was absolutely beautiful.

"Perfect day to stay in bed and watch Christmas movies if the damn power was working."

She looked at me like I'd lost my mind. "Or, ya know, go play in the snow."

"You want to play in the snow?" I questioned.

"Everyone wants to play in the snow, you amoeba."

What did she just call me?

"That's a…weird insult."

"Ehh, it conveyed my point," she defended as she stared out the window. I slapped her ass.

"I may have mentioned it but –"

"I know, I know," she interrupted with an eyeroll. "I'm cuter with something in my mouth."

I walked back over to the bed. "As long as you know."

"I'm sure you'll remind me again if I forget."

I laughed. "You can always count on me."

She twisted her hair into a messy bun, her gaze still fixed out the window.

"I'm going downstairs. Do you want breakfast?" I asked.

"I'll go with you," she offered, closing the curtain.

Someone must have forgotten we have company.

"You do remember that fuckface one and two are down there?"

Her eyes clouded over. "Fuck. I forgot."

I nodded. "I thought you might have. I'll go; you get back in bed."

Looking as if she had lost her best friend, I guess because she really had, she crawled back into bed. The animosity I had for Jace and Cassie grew significantly as I took in the look on her face.

Yeah, they have got to fuckin' go.

Jolene

"Did someone order breakfast in bed?" Dak's voice interrupted my thoughs.

I sat up in bed. "That was fast, chef."

Laughing, he held up two boxes of Poptarts. "Brown sugar or strawberry?"

"Strawberry!"

Wrinkling his nose with judgement, he tossed me the box. "Over brown sugar? That's some questionable decision making."

"I'm a simple girl with simple tastes."

He snorted.

Bitch, I am!

"Were they down there?" I asked quietly.

"They were asleep. He was in the recliner, she was on the couch."

I'm surprised they didn't use the body heat method.

He spoke up, "Don't let them get to you. Mr. Driggers said yesterday that the Department of Transportation salted the roads early to prepare for this weather and that they had snow plows ready to go."

"Okay?"

He smiled. "That means when they wake up, they're gone."

Thank goodness.

"I'm surprised you didn't wake them up when you were down there."

"I thought about it, but I didn't want to start off your snow day with a bunch of hollerin'."

"I appreciate the consideration. I can't believe they actually came here."

He seemed surprised that I felt that way.

"I knew they would."

"I guess I just expected them to go home together after they were caught," I admitted.

He stopped chewing. "What? Why?"

Why wouldn't they?

"They were caught," I pointed out. "They could go home and be together."

He shook his head. "They don't want to be together."

Eying him curiously, I asked, "how do you know that?"

"If they did, they wouldn't be here right now trying to talk to us. They never wanted to be together," he explained. "They wanted to sneak around, to chase the thrill."

"There had to be some part of them that wanted to be together, knowing how much they were risking by doing it."

"It may seem like that, but I don't think so. In fact, I know they didn't want to actually be together."

"How?" I demanded.

"If they loved each other," he began, "I mean, really loved each other, we wouldn't have found out like this."

Now I'm even more confused.

I stared at him waiting for him to explain.

"When you're in love with someone, you don't want to hide it."

"I guess I hadn't thought about it that way."

When you're truly in love with someone, you don't want to hide it...

"If they had wanted to be together, he wouldn't have proposed to you, she wouldn't have accepted when I proposed to her, and we wouldn't be doing this right now. They would have sat us down and told us how they felt."

"But would they, knowing that it would hurt us to hear it?" I pondered more to myself than to him.

"So, the alternative to that would be to do it like this? Knowing damn well that hurting us worse would be the outcome? That doesn't make sense, Loo," he chided gently.

My temper flared. "None of this makes fuckin' sense! We have been planning this wedding for over a year! Y'all's wedding is in, like, four months! So, tell me, what is the goddamn point!?"

He grabbed my arm firmly, hauling me into his lap. "You're not going to be able to understand the actions of a shitty person because you're not a shitty person. You can't relate to how they think."

I relaxed against him. "It's all just so much," I acknowledged tearfully.

"I know but Jack Daniels and I will get you through it."

"That's only while we are here, though," I pointed out. I felt him tense from beneath me.

"What does that mean?"

I shifted in his lap. "We have to go home at some point. Hell, you're supposed to be at work right now."

He cocked his head to the side, thinking over what I had said. "I talked to the chief yesterday and explained what was going on. He already knew, of course, having been at the wedding, but he understands that I just need a few days."

Fabulous. The next year of my life will be spent collecting looks of sympathy from everyone in Creek's Edge.

"Okay."

"We are wastin' a good opportunity by sittin' and talkin' about this."

Are we?

Before I could ask what he meant, he pressed his lips to my neck, and I stopped worrying about talking all together.

Dakota

"I'm pretty sure between you and the whiskey, I'm gonna die of dehydration," Lena joked.

"All I heard is that we provide good service."

She laughed, her naked tits bouncing against my chest.

I stroked her spine. "Are you okay? After the last orgasm, you just kinda collapsed on me."

Sitting up quickly, she stared down at me. "Umm… you kept sayin' to ride you harder, so I was! I thought I was in pretty good shape but after fifteen minutes of riding like that, that check engine light comes on in them knees!"

She did not just say the check engine light.

"Don't be such a girl. You stopped, at least, every three minutes to cum," I teased her. Even though shyness should have been long gone since she was currently completely naked and straddling me, she blushed. "Hush! You make my body freeze like it's taking a screenshot when I cum, so I have to stop bouncin' for it!"

Grinning from ear to ear, I spoke up, "Again, all I heard is that I'm providing good service."

Nodding enthusiastically, she reached out to fist bump. "Thanks for the good lay, Lieutenant!"

A fist bump…

I pulled her back down onto my chest. Turning her head sideways, she asked quietly, "Do you think they're still down there?"

"If they are, we need to charge them admission because you really gave them a show." My exhausted cock tingled as I recalled the sounds she had made.

"You hollered out a few times, too!"

"I did," I admitted. "A few times, but you, ma'am, are very vocal when you're havin' a good time."

"It be like that sometimes," she joked. "At least, that's what I've learned in the last few days."

Jolene

I want a fuckin' shower.

Dak looked up from the ancient book he was reading. "Why are you makin' that face?"

"I was thinkin' about how much I want a shower," I confessed.

Closing the book, he sat up. "If they salted the roads, we could try to head back to Creek's Edge."

Already?

"Yeah, we could. Are you sure the roads will be okay?"

"I'll call Chief and see how it looks on the home side before we leave," he promised. "First things first, I'm goin' to see if they're still here."

I watched him leave the room in nothing but his boxers. Not wanting to hear any of the exchange, I got up to close the door. With nothing else to do, I walked around the room blowing out all the candles.

How am I gonna get all my crap from Jace's house?

"Why can't I be rich enough to just leave it and replace everything?" I groaned out loud.

"Because God couldn't make you this pretty and rich. It would be showing favoritism," Dak explained.

I whirled around. "I didn't hear you come in."

"That's because you were talkin' to yourself, ya little nutjob."

"I was thinkin' out loud!" I defended myself.

He started stripping sheets from the bed. "Whatever you say, loony toon."

I pulled the pillows from the cases. "Were they down there?"

Crumpling the sheets into a ball, he tossed them on the floor. "Yes. I told them to get out. I told them we are leavin' in four hours and that he better have your stuff packed and waiting and that she needed to go get her shit out of my house."

I felt my eyes widen. "You're kickin' her out?"

He looked at me like I was speaking a different language. "Of course, I am. Did you think I was goin' to let her stay?"

I mean, kinda…

"I figured you'd forgive her. You just needed to be mad first."

He wrinkled his nose in disgust. "Are you going to forgive him?"

I thought it over for a moment. "No."

He sighed. "I'll forgive them both because I don't deserve the burden of what comes with holdin' onto it, but I ain't gonna forget and she ain't stayin' in my house."

"Did they agree to what you asked them to do?"

He made a noise that was somewhere between a scoff and a laugh. "I didn't ask them. I told them… but they both nodded their heads."

Jace is going to throw all my shit out into the yard.

"I hope he doesn't mess up all my stuff. All my stuff is there for my candle business."

"He won't mess up your things. Destruction of property would cost him his job at the fire department. He knows he's already lost enough," he promised.

I tried to believe him. "Okay. Why did you tell him we weren't leaving for four hours?"

He grinned. "I believe someone wanted a snow day."

Dakota

"You're sure Chief said the roads weren't bad?" Lena asked for the tenth time.

"He said they were fine. He said they had only responded to one accident, and it was a single car DUI. No weather related events."

She fidgeted nervously. "Do we leave the food on the back porch or take it with us?

"Chief said three to four more inches are comin' this way tomorrow so I guess we will take it with us. I don't want to put it in the fridge, and have it spoil because we don't know when the power will be back on."

"Damn, more snow?"

I nodded. "That's what Chief said."

"I'll go grab the stuff off the porch!"

"While you do that, I'll go get the rest of our stuff loaded up." As she headed out the back door, I walked out the front. Ten minutes later, I was walkin' back across the yard, everything loaded up and ready to go.

That candle bag is entirely too damn heavy for her to be carrying around.

I slipped inside the front door. "Loo, ya ready?"

No response.

I walked to the back door. There she stood at the picnic table, slowly putting things into a bag.

She's definitely stalling.

I slip open the door. "How are you still baggin' stuff up? It was only like eight things. I already put your stuff in your car, my stuff in my truck and I'm already done. And let's not forget I had to walk fifteen miles to your car to start with because of who you are as a person."

She shot me a dirty look. "I wanted to pack it neatly."

I tossed some sandwich meat into the bag. "I'm sure it's fine. I'm gonna go upstairs and double check that the fire is out, and I'll meet you in the living room."

"Okay," she answered quietly.

Maybe she doesn't want to leave?

After making sure the fireplace was flame free, I met her at the kitchen counter. "Okay, girlie pop. Let's go!" I picked the bag of food up from the top of the counter.

As we stepped out onto the front porch, my mood took an immediate nosedive.

Reality really is a bitch.

We walked past our freshly built snowman in silence, our feet crunching against the thick snow.

"I'll walk you to your car. Take the food with you and donate it to that women's shelter next to the bank." She nodded but she looked like she was close to tears.

I stopped her dead in her tracks. "Lena?"

"Hmmm?" she mumbled, never taking her eyes off the ground.

"What's wrong?"

"Nothing," she mumbled.

Bullshit.

"Jolene."

She said nothing.

"If you don't want to go," I began, "we can stay. I just know we are both ready to wash our ass."

Still refusing to look away from the packed snow, she spoke up. "I'm okay with leavin'. I do want a shower. I just… are you sure Chief Hennessy said the roads are okay?" The anxiety in her voice was palpable.

She's afraid to drive back alone because of the weather.

"He said they're fine, but I'll tell you what, I'll drive us back in my truck. We can just leave your car here and I'll bring you to get it this comin' weekend."

Relief flickered across her face before fleeing just as quickly. "I can't. I have to get my stuff from Jace's house," she explained.

Oh, no ma'am.

"You're not goin' to get your stuff, anyways," I informed her. "I'm goin' to get it."

She looked shocked. "You are? Why?"

Cause I'm prayin' he grows a pair and tries me so I can fuck him the hell up.

"Because you said you didn't want to deal with him, and I want to make sure you don't have to."

She smiled gratefully. "In that case, let's go!"

Jolene

The forty-five-minute ride with Dakota back to Creek's Edge was fun but I felt the tears threatening the second I saw the city limit sign.

Dak noticed the sudden tension in the air. "When you get to your parents' house and take a shower, lay down and take a nap."

I don't want a nap.

"Why?"

"Because the adrenaline from being in survival mode the last few days is goin' to wear off and bitch slap you. It will make you feel like crap."

I stared out the window. "I haven't felt any adrenaline from this. I feel anger."

"Anger fuels adrenaline. Anger fuels a lot of things."

I didn't respond. It seemed more polite to remain silent than it did to tell him I thought he was crazy.

"I know you think I'm wrong, but would you and I have ever had sex under normal circumstances?"

I bit my lip, thinking it over. "Absolutely not."

He threw his hand up as if I'd said exactly what he wanted me to say. "I rest my case. Adrenaline."

We drove the rest of the way in silence, the only sound between us was the song Brooks and Dunn were singing on the radio.

As he pulled up in my parents' yard, he reached over and rubbed the top of my thigh. "This is the part I was referring to when I said it's gonna get worse. A lot of people are goin' to be talkin'. Ignore that shit."

I nodded.

He stopped the truck in the spot my daddy appointed to him back when we were in high school.

The memory made me smile. "Remember when daddy told you if you messed up his grass again by driving across it, he would spike the food with exlax then invite you over for supper?"

He gave me a deadpanned look. "Why do you think I'm still parkin' exactly where he told me to park nearly two decades later?"

I laughed. "Mama wouldn't have let him mess with y'all's food."

He swung open his truck door. "I wasn't takin' no chances."

Shaking my head, I hopped out of his truck. We trekked through the rare Georgia snow with an awkward silence settling between us. Both of us were unsure of what to say so we both just stared straight ahead. Thankfully, my mama, who could always be counted upon, came barreling out of the front door.

"Lee Lee! Dak!"

She embraced him for a quick minute before throwing her arms around my neck, lingering just long enough for a lump to start to form in my throat.

"Hey, Mama."

She pulled away but held me at arm's length. "I'm so sorry, sugar." She turned to face Dakota. "For both of y'all. I'm so sorry," her voice wavered, evidence that she was fighting back tears.

My mama had been like a second mama to Cassie since we were in elementary school and to the boys since we were in high school. She had always loved and treated all of them the same way she did me and my brother, coining her the nickname "Mama C" a long, long time ago. I knew without a doubt that, while it was for a very different reason, her heart was just as broken by all of this as mine and Dakota's.

Dak put his arm around her. "Look on the bright side, Mama C, now you… I mean, Santa… has two less stockings to fill this year for Christmas."

Damn, I forgot Christmas is in less than two weeks.

Mama smiled sadly. "Y'all hungry? I didn't know y'all would be back today, but I always cook enough for an army. I have

homemade vegetable soup in the Crockpot if y'all want some."
Dak's eyes lit up immediately, his reaction answering for the both of us.

"Perfect!" She beamed. "C'mon in, the house is good and warm."

That's a good thing, Mama, because the world is fuckin' cold.

Dakota

Being in the Felder house would always be my favorite place to be. Having a dad that owned a bank branch and a mama that chose meth over me a long time ago, the place that I always felt most at home was this house.

My dad has always been a great man, but he spent most of my teen years married to his work, determined to make our name known for something other than the sins and scandals my mama left behind. Lena's mama is the only true maternal figure I have ever had, and I am smart enough to know she is the main reason I became a firefighter and not a felon. My daddy taught me to work hard to succeed and, especially, to prove people wrong, but it was Mr. Brett, Lena's daddy, that actually forced me to develop a work ethic.

Most teenage boys spent their summers chasing tail they'd never actually get or riding the town strip with their friends, but not us. Mr. Brett had me, Jace, and Lena's brother, Cruise spending our summer breaks right here, helping him out with the farm every day. We were compensated, of course, with a paycheck that seemed huge to us back then, a permanent spot at Mama C's supper table, and more dips in their backyard pool than a man could count. I didn't realize it back then but what I gained from those years of manual labor was a work ethic that would carry me the rest of my life, while also giving me the desire to always help out someone if I had the opportunity to do it.

Mama C gestured towards the living room. "Y'all go sit a spell. I'll bring y'all a bowl of soup."

After removing our shoes in the entryway, we obeyed her command, both of us electing the reclining sectional as our landing zone.

"If you need to get home to Athens, Mama will understand," Lena spoke up.

I shook my head. "Athens is having the time of her life out at Papa Jake's house. She's probably snoozing in his recliner or licking the windows to try to get a taste of the snow. Besides, I want some vegetable soup."

She smiled and looked out the window. "It's perfect weather for the soup. I can't believe Creek's Edge actually got a measurable amount of snow. The mountains are one thing, but I think it's snowed, maybe, five times here our whole life."

"Chief said that the last time we got this much snow was in the seventies," I informed her.

"He's right!" Mama C chimed in from the doorway. "In 1973, we got a bunch. Around a foot or so." She passed each of us a bowl of soup, a napkin, and a spoon. "Y'all go ahead and take this. I'll be right back."

Inhaling appreciatively, I grinned at Lena. "You need to figure out how to turn this exact smell into a candle." She looked up, her pretty face covered in confusion. "The smell of vegetable soup?"

"Not exactly the soup, but just the smell of this house, especially this time of the year."

The Felder house in December always smelled of delicious food, pine needles, cinnamon, apples, and just…clean.

"I wouldn't even know how to replicate it," she confessed.

Mama returned with a plate of cornbread and two glasses of sweet tea. "Replicate what?"

"The smell of your house," Lena explained. "Dak told me I needed to make it into a candle."

Mama laughed. "Actually, all the smells in here, except the soup and whatever smells that seep from the laundry room, are from those wax melts you gave me to test out, Lee Lee."

She does wax melts, too?

"I didn't know you did wax melts, too."

Lena slurped her soup. "I don't. Not yet, anyway. It was something I was trying out because Jace was lecturing me about how candles are unsafe."

What?

"How candles are unsafe?"

She snagged a piece of cornbread from the plate Mama had sat between us. "He said candles are a fire hazard so no one would buy them."

Her mama's mouth dropped open in horror but all I could do was shake my damn head. "He shouldn't have told you that mess. By all intents and purposes, everything is a fire hazard."

"He's right," her mama offered. "Donna and Fletcher Collins' barn burned down from a bird's nest that was up inside the light globe."

Lena looked up, her expression calling bullshit on the Collins. "I have never heard of such."

"They hadn't, either!" Mama exclaimed. Lena and I exchanged glances. We both knew it was likely their grandson, the secret pot smoker, who burnt down the barn rather than the pigeons, but neither of us were about to tell her that.

I blew on another spoonful of soup. "This is delicious, Mama." She beamed. "I'm glad you're enjoyin' it!"

The sound of the front door shutting startled us.

I didn't even hear it open.

Mr. Brett walked in the room, his eyes lighting up the instant he saw his daughter. Ignoring his wife's "no shoes throughout the house" rule, he and his dirty boots traipsed into the living room.

After sitting her bowl of soup on the side table, Lena rose to greet him. "Hey, Daddy."

He folded her into his arms, his shoulders visibly relaxing as he squeezed her.

"I'm so glad you are home, Lee Lee," he spoke warmly, "I was worried about you."

She squeezed tighter. "I'm okay."

Above her head, his eyes teared up. His wife noticed it, too, interjecting quickly to make sure Lena didn't. "Alright, Brett. Let the child eat. I'll go fix you a bowl."

Knowing it was in his best interest to listen to his wife, he released Lena.

"You're the best, Charlie Girl," he praised his wife as he reached out to shake my hand.

"How ya doin', Mr. B?"

"Hardheaded but above ground," he joked. "How are you doin', bud?"

"Takin' it day by day."

Nodding, he sat down in his recliner. "That's all you can do."

Mama returned with his bowl of soup. "If you want this soup, you're gonna have to get them wet, nasty boots off my carpet."

Standing up immediately, he headed straight for the front door to abandon his boots. From the other side of the sectional, Lena watched her parents quietly, clearly thinking the same thing that I was thinking.

We weren't askin' too much. We were askin' the wrong people.

Jolene

"Turn your phone back on so I can reach you," Dakota demanded. "Ignore or delete anything that upsets you, but please keep it on so I can check on you."

We had just finished our soup and the last half of a Hallmark Christmas movie when he announced he needed to get going. Now, we were standing next to his truck, making sure I had gotten all of my things out.

"I'll cut it on," I promised. "It probably needs charging."

Reaching into his truck, he grabbed the orange charger he unnecessarily bought while we were in the mountains. "Here. Go plug it in."

Quit bossing me around, my guy.

As badly as I wanted to remind him that I am a grown ass woman, I knew his constant state of overbearingness was coming from a good place.

"Yes, daddy," I joked. His eyes clouded over.

It was a joke.

He suddenly looked uncomfortable.

"What's the matter?"

He propped his elbow up on the bed of his truck. "I don't know how to say goodbye to you now."

You what, now?

"You open your mouth, and if you try to speak really, really hard, words come out."

He rolled his eyes. "I'm serious."

"What do you mean? Why?"

He ran his fingers through his hair and sighed. "Well, you know Cassie and I have been together since high school…," he trailed off.

I narrowed my eyes. "Okay?"

Where is he going with this?

"That means she's the only person that I've ever slept with and I always kissed her goodbye… now that you and I have slept together, I don't know if I should kiss you goodbye, too, because anything less might be insulting or if I should just high five you or something." He looked genuinely stressed.

I laughed, hoping it would lighten the mood, but he just looked more worked up.

"Do not kiss me. We slept together under extenuating circumstances, not because we are in a relationship." He looked relieved. "Hugs are still okay, though, right?"

Rolling my eyes, I threw my arms around his neck. "Hugs are still okay, moron."

He relaxed as he held me, the moment lasting longer than it should. After kissing me on the top of my head, he released me. "Go plug your phone in and wash your nasty ass. I'll drop your stuff off tonight."

"I'm going. Don't do anything stupid when you go to his house."

He scoffed.

"I'm serious, Dakota. Promise me." I held out my pinky.

He shot me a death glare but he pinky promised anyway.

Relieved, I walked towards the front porch. "Call me if you need me," I called out over my shoulder.

Leaning against the front porch column, I watched him pull out the driveway, suddenly feeling lonelier than I had ever felt in my life.

Dakota

"This motherfucker better have all her shit packed up," I said to myself as I pulled up in Jace's yard.

There was a small part of me that was surprised that Cassie's car wasn't in the driveway.

After parking as close as I could get to the front porch without winding up on top of his rocking chairs, I climbed out of the truck. I had promised myself I was going to stay calm, but I could feel my anger mounting as I banged on his front door. "Open up, Reynolds!"

Dressed in only his boxers, he opened the door, never uttering a word before turning his back to walk away. He sat down in his chair, reclining it back before pointing a finger towards a bunch of containers next to the fireplace. "That's all of it, except her work clothes. They're laying across the dining room table because they're all on hangers."

I watched as he lifted a crystal tumbler of brown liquid to his lips. I wanted to knock his ass out the damn chair, but as I took in the dark circles under his eyes, his thick stubble and his disheveled hair, I knew he was suffering already. That satisfied me enough.

For now.

"'Preciate it." I spoke curtly.

Saying nothing, he swilled from his tumbler. I grabbed three totes, making the decision to haul them out to the porch first and then, to my truck. About halfway through the moving process, he spoke up quietly. "Do you need help?"

"It'll get me out of here quicker."

Tossing back the rest of his drink, he pushed up off the chair. "Quicker means you can get back to fuckin' my fiancé faster, right?"

I know damn well this motherfucker didn't just say that to me.

I laughed sarcastically. "Hey kettle, this is the pot. You're black."

"I never denied that I fucked up, but two wrongs don't make a right," he defended himself. I grabbed the tote with Lena's candle supplies. "See, the interesting part of that statement is that it's often used out of context. This is one of those times."

He sat the container he was holding on the front steps. "Actually, it's not."

I walked back inside to grab the last tote.

Don't engage in this because you're goin' to wind up gettin' your ass in trouble.

From the doorway, he stared at me, waiting for me to argue with him.

"Lena and I are both single and free to do whatever we want. You and Cassie, however, were not single. You were both engaged and planning weddings to other people."

He stepped out onto the porch so I could get through. "Still don't make it right."

After stacking two containers on top of each other, I put them in the bed of my truck.

"You're speaking on right and wrong…after gettin' caught railing your fiancé's best friend…in a church… on your wedding day. Not sure your moral compass points in the direction that earns you the position to speak on right and wrong."

I continued loading up Lena's stuff. Neither of us said a word as I arranged the containers in the bed of my truck, making sure that nothing could get messed up or broken.

I was getting ready to leave when I remembered I had forgotten to grab her work clothes.

He followed me into the house, looking as if he wanted to cry. "I made a mistake," he confessed quietly.

I grabbed her hanging clothes from the dining room table. "The sad thing is, you say you made a mistake, but you don't even mean doin' what you did to start with. You mean you made a mistake by gettin' caught."

That remark struck a nerve, and he shoved me, angrily, damn near sending my unsuspecting ass through the front windows.

Fuck him up, Dakota.

Every part of me wanted to knock his head up against every wall in his house, but nothing about this fucking idiot was worth jeopardizing my career.

Steadying myself, I walked out the front door, holding the last bit of her that he had in my hands. I walked to the passenger side of my truck, Jace hot on my heels, determined to ignore his attempt to provoke me. I started laying her clothes out across my back seat, growing more and more irritated with how brave he decided he wanted to be today.

 He was standing behind me near the bed of the truck, but still close enough that I could feel the heat coming off of his body.

"Back up off me, Reynolds," I warned, closing the truck's back door. He didn't back up, but instead, he moved closer. "You gonna do something about it, Clayton? Or just run your mouth?"

Don't take the bait, Dak. He's trying to make himself feel better by getting you to stoop to his level.

I laughed hard, an honest to goodness laugh that my body must have been holding back.

This motherfucker.

His outrage grew when I turned to walk away.

I promised her I would behave.

He followed me from one side of the Chevy to the other, popping off at the mouth before shoving me chest first into the driver side.

"I wouldn't get too comfortable with your new piece of ass 'cause she will be back in my bed by the end of the week," he taunted.

I can always get a new job.

Spinning around, I grabbed him by the throat. Glass went flying as I slammed him against the driver's door. "Let's get one goddamn thing straight, motherfucker. If I catch you anywhere near her, I will fuckin' kill you. You can go ahead and call Hennessy and tell him I threatened you if you want to, but you can tell him I said that it's not a threat. It's a fuckin' promise. I will fuckin' kill you, Jace. Do you understand me?"

I tightened my grip around his throat, a silent dare to get him to try to say something crazy.

He wisely chose to stay silent.

Using the grasp I had on his neck, I threw him on the ground.

He knew enough to know he had better not try to get up.

"You're pathetic, Jace. And just like every other cheating piece of shit, you realized what you had in front of you way too late."

Ignoring the glass, I climbed in my truck. "And by that point, she was waking up next to someone that already knew."

I slammed the door, sending more glass flying, but I was too fucking pissed off to care.

The last thing I saw as I pulled out of his yard was the dumb fuck climbing up out of the snow.

Jolene

There's something to be said for a good, hot shower.

I combed through my long, wet hair.

It feels so weird to be back at home.

I braided my hair Elsa style before realizing I had nothing to secure it. I was rummaging around my bathroom vanity when there was a knock at the door.

"Lee Lee?"

"Come on in, Mama."

She opened the door with a worried look on her face. "Feelin' any better, sugar?"

I do, actually.

"Yes, ma'am. The power was out at the cabin the whole time we were at the cabin, so I haven't showered since before the… well, you know."

She stroked my cheek. "I know, sweetie. Dak explained the power was out when he called Sunday. Your daddy was so relieved to find out he was with you up there. We both were," she admitted.

I hung up my towel on the door hook. "I didn't know he was comin' up there," I told her. "As bad as it sounds, when I ran out of the church, Dakota never even crossed my mind."

You're selfish as fuck, Lena.

"That's understandable though, Lee. You were in shock."

"I know," I agreed. "I do feel bad for it, though, because he's been such a good friend these last few days."

"He's always been good friend," she reminded me.

He really has.

She fixed the strings on my hoodie. "Have you talked to either of them?" she asked gently.

"They came to the cabin."

"What!?"

I nodded. "Can we go talk in my room? It's hot in here." Her eyes crinkled as if she had forgotten we were standing in my steamy bathroom.

"Oh, yes, of course!" She held open the bathroom door. "C'mon, you have to explain all that to me!"

Once we were in my room, we climbed on my bed the way we used to do when I was a teenager.

"Okay, spill it, sister!"

On today's episode of Gossip Girl.

"Okay, so, on Sunday night, Dakota and I were in the hot tub."

She raised an eyebrow.

"Nothin' like that," I lied quickly. "It was freezing, and the hot tub was warm. We had no power, remember?"

She looked confused. "How was the hot tub working, then?"

"It has a battery backup."

"Ahh, okay. Go on," she instructed. I laughed.

"So, we are in the hot tub, and I heard someone callin' my name from inside the house."

She covered her mouth. "No!"

"Yes, girl!"

Damn, I've missed gossiping with my Mama.

"What happened, then?"

"Dakota and I went inside, and it was Jace and Cassie."

"And!?" she prompted.

"And nothin' really. Jace insisted on talkin' to me, but Dak told him if he came near me, he would take him to a place that made hell seem like a happy place."

Her eyes widened. "Ya know, I'm not even surprised. Dakota knocked the fire outta him at the church."

I nodded. "He was tellin' me about that."

She rubbed her temples. "I was so focused on makin' sure your daddy didn't hit him that it never even occurred to me that Dak might deck him."

I curled up with my pillow. "What happened after I left the church?" She kicked back next to me. "After you ran out, I went to get your daddy because I thought you might need a ride. I knew you had ridden to the church with me. By the time I explained to him what was happening, you were gone."

I giggled. "I saw that Jace had driven my car instead of his truck. Once I realized the keys were still in, I hauled tail."

"I know!" She laughed. "After Dak found out and knocked Jace on his behind, your daddy and I went into the sanctuary to explain that the wedding wouldn't be happening that day and thanked everyone for comin'."

"That day or any other day," I muttered. She smiled sympathetically. "Your daddy and I didn't know what you would decide to do in the future."

"Y'all thought I might stay with him?"" I asked incredulously.

"We didn't know, sugar. Your daddy was hellbent against it, but you make your own decisions."

I stared at my childhood bedroom ceiling.

Clearly, I make poor decisions.

"I just feel so silly, Mama."

She stroked my hair.

"I feel like I was too stupid to see the signs. Hell, I still can't see the signs and I have been wrackin' my brain for days now tryin' to see them."

"Oh, honey, you wouldn't have been able to see the signs because you never expected to find them in two of the people you loved most in the world."

The tears I had been fighting back for days finally gave up.

Allowing myself to finally feel the pain, I curled up in my Mama's arms and cried for the little girl that knew she didn't deserve this.

Dakota

What the fuck is she doin' here?

Cassie's Ford Escape sat parked in my garage as if it were a week ago and she was actually supposed to be here.

I grabbed my keys and my phone.

I need to clean up this glass.

After closing the garage door, I walked in the side door. I was already pissed off about what happened at Jace's house and even more annoyed now that I have to deal with her.

"Cassie!" I bellowed, my voice echoing off the hardwood floors. She walked out on the second-floor balcony wearing a black robe. "Dakota! You're home!"

I am home. You are not and you need to go.

"Come down here, Cassie," I ordered. Even from the ground floor, I could see that she wanted to argue but decided against it. She came down the stairs quietly, her gaze locked on her feet.

"Didn't I tell you to have your stuff out before I got home? What are you still doin' here?

She fidgeted with her hands. "I needed to talk to you."

"It would be impossible for me to overstate how little I care about anything you have to say."

She smirked. "Okay, you win. No talkin'." She dropped the robe, revealing her completely naked body underneath. She was tanned, toned, and curvy in all the right places.

And yet, I've never been more turned off in my life.

Bending over, I picked up the satin robe and wrapped in around her. "Can you please try to find a shred of self-respect?"

Pouting, she batted her long eyelashes. "You know you want me, Dakota. You've never been able to resist me," she purred, sliding her hands across my chest. I caught her by her wrists.

"You're right, Cass," I agreed. "I've never been able to resist you."

She smiled triumphantly, moving closer to try and press her body against mine. Leaning down, I pressed my lips against her ear. "But there's a first time for everything and you and your community cunt need to get the fuck outta my house." Dropping her wrist, I turned and walked towards the door. "I'm goin' to take Lena her stuff. When I get back, you better be gone."

The last thing I heard before slamming the door was her calling my name. I backed out of my garage, my tires spinning on the gravel.

I have never wanted to leave my own damn house until this moment.

"Hey, Siri," I summoned. "Call Loo."

The ringing came through my truck's speakers.

No answer.

She better be napping.

Deciding on a last-minute change of plans, I turned off the main street into the back parking lot of the fire department. Some of the guys from my shift were out there shooting hoops. After parking in the lieutenant's spot, I climbed out, careful to avoid shards of glass. All at once, I was swarmed with first bumps and one-armed hugs, the guy's faces painted with sympathy.

Carter spoke up first. "You look good, DK. How you doin', buddy?" He slapped me on the shoulder.

"Doin' good."

They all exchanged looks

"Don't do all that. I'm good, really," I promised. "He did me a favor."

The rookie, Dedric, who I had grown rather fond of, gave me a bear hug. "More fish in the sea, dawg."

I nodded. "Is Chief inside?"

Zeke sunk a perfect swish. "He's in there. He's making his five-alarm chili."

"Aight, I'll be back." They resumed their game as I walked into the truck bay.

"How you holdin' up, Lieu?"

What? Lena's here?

I looked around quickly.

Ben Dakes walked out from behind one of the engines.

He was talkin' to you, dumbass.

"One day at a time."

"I heard that. Holler if you need anything!" He fist bumped me.

"Will do. Thanks, man."

I found the chief in the station's kitchen chopping up peppers to put in his chili.

"DK! I didn't know you were back. How are ya, kid?"

"Good, good, Chief. I just needed to talk to you a minute."

He scraped the diced peppers into a pot of sauce.

"I'm always here to listen, but you know I can't choose sides between two of my best guys. I don't agree with what Jace did at all and I'm going to tell him my piece when I see him, but I won't get involved beyond so long as you two don't do anything stupid."

Well, it might be a little too late for that.

"I understand that. I just wanted to let you know it won't affect me on the job. I know Reynolds was supposed to move from B Shift to my rotation next week."

He looked surprised. "I was just goin' to leave him where he was at for now. I know you are both professionals, but it just seemed like the best option right this minute with everything goin' on."

"I think I can speak for both of us when I say that we won't allow any of this to impact our professional relationship."

He nodded slowly. "I'll think on it and speak to Jace when he comes back."

I absentmindedly stirred the chili. "Yes, sir."

He began chopping jalapenos. "How is Lena doin'?"

I exhaled. "She's okay, I think. Back at her parents."

"I imagine Brett is relieved to have her home."

"I'm sure he is. Speakin' of that, I gotta head over there now. I picked up her stuff from Jace's and I need to drop it off."

"Tell her I asked about her, will ya? Tell her she better not be a stranger around here now. This will all sort itself out in the wash."

"I'll tell her, Chief."

After telling him I'd be back tomorrow for my shift, I headed to Lena's house.

Jolene

"Lee Lee?" Mama shook me gently.

I opened one eye to squint at her.

"Dakota is downstairs," she spoke gently.

"Actually, Dakota is upstairs," he called out from the doorway. "Mr. B gave me permission!"

Mama and I both laughed.

It was a well-established rule in our teens that boys were not allowed upstairs for any reason. Because both Jace and Dakota knew better than to test my daddy so neither of them have ever been in my room.

I yawned. "Hey, Dak."

"Hey, Lena Loo!" He greeted me cheerfully. "I have your stuff."

"You went to Jace's and got her things?" Mama questioned him.

"Yes, ma'am. She said she didn't want to see him, so I told her I'd go."

Mama patted his arm appreciatively. "Thanks, Dakota. You likely saved Ole Brett from an assault charge."

Dak laughed. "It was no trouble at all."

Mama walked out into the hallway. "Y'all behave… or don't."

That's subtle, Mama.

I rolled over in bed to face him.

"Hey buddy."

"Hey pal," he responded, sitting down on the edge of my bed.

"Uh oh, Brett gonna get yo' ass for bein' on my bed," I teased.

"I'll take my chances." He kicked back against my headboard. "I see you actually listened."

I did?

"If I did, it was purely by accident," I assured him.

He rolled his eyes. "You took a nap."

"Oh yeah, I did. Felt great, too."

He smiled. "I'm glad to hear it. I still haven't even showered yet."

What has he been doin' all day?

"Damn, it must have taken awhile to grab my stuff. I'm sorry," I apologized.

He shook his head. "Nah, it only took about thirty minutes. He had it all packed up in totes."

How considerate.

"I'm kinda shocked. I didn't expect either of them to do what you asked."

"Well, you're half right."

You can't be half right. You're either right or you're wrong.

"Half right, how?"

"After I got finished at Jace's house, I went home…" he trailed off. "Cassie was at the house."

Ahh, half right about them listening.

"Still packin' her stuff up?"

He ran his fingers through his hair. "Not exactly."

"She hadn't packed? Was she hopin' you had changed your mind and decided to let her stay?"

"She tried to convince me to let her stay."

Shocking.

I waited patiently for him to explain.

"When I got home," he began, "she didn't have on anything except a silk robe… which she dropped…and, yeah."

And…yeah? And, yeah what?

"Oh, shit."

"Yeah." He stood up. "I'm gonna go grab your stuff outta the truck."

I was irritated for reasons I couldn't explain.

After all this, he slept with her because she was wearin' nothin' but a robe?

I knew the robe he was referring to. I was with her when she bought it.

"I can come help." I pulled back my covers. "Just let me get on some pants."

I stood up wearing only a huge T-shirt and a pair of panties.

"No, I'll get it. You stay here." he ordered, never taking is eyes off the bedroom door.

He didn't even look at me when I said I didn't have on pants.

"Are you sure?" I asked. "I don't mind helping."

He waved me off. "I'll be back."

Within seconds, I heard him clopping down the staircase.

"Why is he actin' completely different than he was actin' in the mountains?" I said softly to myself.

And why is it bothering me so much?

Dakota

I stepped out the Felder's front door to find Mr. Brett taping a trash bag to my driver's window.

"Looks like you had an interesting time today, son," he remarked.

"Yes, sir."

He shook his head. "Listen, Dakota," he started, "I wanted to beat his ass, too, but ain't worth you losin' everything you've built for yourself down at the station."

Mr. Brett very rarely called me by my first name, usually only when he's really saying something he wanted me to really hear.

"I know you're right," I admitted. "I just want to make him feel all the pain he's caused her."

He finished taping the window. "Trust me, I get it. That's my baby girl," he spoke fondly." But I learned a long time ago that karma will take care of those that fuck you over and if you're lucky, you'll be around to watch."

I'm a lot quicker than karma, Mr. B.

"Yes, sir. Thank you… for the window and the advice."

He slapped me on the shoulder. "You're a good fella, Dak. Don't stop bein' that way because of somebody else."

I nodded.

He gestured towards the bed of the truck. "All this Lee Lee's?"

I lifted two containers "Yes, sir. Hopefully, it's all of it. Jace packed it up."

"Waste of air, that kid," he muttered under his breath as he lifted a few totes.

Together, we made trip after trip up the stairs, arranging her stuff neatly in her bedroom.

She was no longer relaxing in bed; she had joined her mama at the kitchen island.

"Coffee?" I teased her. "It's dark outside!"

"I drink coffee all day long," she reminded me.

Coffee and showers. The obsessions of Lena.

Mama C handed me a cup of coffee. "Here, honey. It'll warm you up," she informed me. "Make sure you get that window fixed before you catch pneumonia."

"Window?" Lena piped up. "What window?"

Thanks, Mama.

I ran my fingers through my oily hair. "The window on the driver's door of my truck got knocked out," I explained hesitantly.

Her eyes widened. "What?" Sitting her cup of coffee on the island, she jumped off her stool and sprinted toward the front door.

Sighing, I stared up at the ceiling.

Mr. Brett put his coffee mug in the sink. "Both of the Felder woman are motor mouths. She ran out there with no shoes on."

I sat down my mug. "I'll take her some shoes."

Grabbing her hunting boots from the entryway shelf, I followed her out the front door.

She was standing at my truck surveying the damage. "Dakota! What the fuck happened?!" she hollered out.

Girl, your mama gonna wash your mouth out with soap.

I pressed my fingers to my lips reminding her that it wasn't just us in the general area. "Watch your mouth!" I hissed. "Your mama might be able to hear us."

Guiltily, she ducked behind the driver's door. "Fuck!" she whispered. "What happened?"

Nothin' compared to what could have happened.

"Jace and I had a little…riff… but it wasn't bad and everything is fine."

"Everything is fine? There's glass all over your truck, Dakota!"

No shit, Sherlock.

"I know it," I told her calmly. "Put these on."

She snatched her boots from me and slid them on.

"Well, come on!"

Come on where, crazy lady?

"Where to?"

She threw her hands up in frustration and spoke to me as if I were a child. "We are going to the corner store so we can vacuum all this glass out of your damn seat!"

I shook my head. "I'll get it later."

She had already climbed up into the passenger side. "Get the fuck in the truck, Dakota," she ordered.

Knowing she wasn't going to let this go, I got the fuck in the truck.

Jolene

"How long have you been drivin' around with glass stuck to your ass?" I demanded.

He pulled out of my parents' driveway. "Only a few hours. I forgot there was glass in here, honestly."

Dumbfounded, I stared at him. "You are completely crazy." I picked a few chunks of glass out of the cupholder, tossing them into the floor.

"How did the window wind up shattered?"

"We kinda got into a tussle and I slammed him against the truck."

I shook my head. "Y'all are both gonna lose your jobs for actin' like that," I pointed out.

"Nah." He pulled into the gas station. "I already talked to the chief."

As he stopped at the industrial vacuum, I hopped out of the truck.

"I can vacuum it out. Get back in the truck."

Why are you so damn bossy?

"I wanna help!"

He leaned down to my eye level. "You are half fuckin' dressed and there is snow on the damn ground. Get. Your. Ass. In. The. Truck."

I looked down at my oversized t-shirt, pajama shorts, and insulated boots.

I am fully dressed. I'm not dressed great, but I am dressed.

I folded my arms stubbornly. "I'm dressed fine," I shot back. "And I want to help."

"You can get in the truck, or I can put you in the truck," he threatened.

Putting my hands on my hips, I called his bluff. "I don't have to listen to you, bro. I'm a grown woman."

In one quick swoop, I was laying over his shoulder.

"Put me down!"

He opened the passenger door. "I am!" He dropped me on the seat. "Stay," he told me before slamming the door.

"I'm not a fuckin' dog, Dakota!" I shouted at him through the open driver's door.

Ignoring me, he shoved quarters into the vacuum cleaner. The machine sputtered a bit before waking up but eventually found a rhythm. He dragged the hose to where he needed it to be, the sudden sound of glass being sucked up, filling the cab.

Missed a spot.

He slid his seat forward and backward, making sure he got every nook and cranny. He finished fairly quickly; the only remaining evidence of their "riff" was the Glad Force Flex taped to the window frame.

We drove back to my parent's house in silence, neither of us sure of what to say.

It's safe to say that our little rendezvous in the mountains fucked our friendship all the way up.

He parked in his spot like he'd done a thousand times before. Unbuckling my seatbelt, I twisted in my seat to face him. "Comin' inside?"

He stared straight ahead. "Nah, I'm gonna head home. I have to work tomorrow."

"Okay. Stay safe." I opened the door.

"Always. Tell your parents I said goodnight."

I nodded my head before climbing out. "Okay." When he didn't turn to look at me, I shut the door.

I held back tears as I walked to the porch.

In the last four days, I'd lost my fiancé and two of my best friends.

And I have no idea where the fuck to go from here.

223

Dakota

Cassie's car was still in my garage.

Why did I think for even a split second that she would make this easy.

I walked through the side door to find three boxes next to the kitchen island.

Maybe she decided to act like she has some sense.

"Dak, is that you?" she called out from upstairs.

Who else would it be?

"Yes."

She appeared at the top of the stairs wearing Christmas pajamas.

At least she has clothes on this time.

"I'm tryin' to pack. I just have a lot of stuff," she whimpered.

"Okay. It's gettin' late. Just finish tomorrow while I'm at work."

Her eyes lit up. "Okay, thank you."

As I climbed the staircase, I refused to look at her. When I reached the top, she reached out for me. "Can we please talk?"

I do not want to talk to you.

"I'm goin' to bed. I have to work tomorrow," I spoke brusquely. "You can sleep in the guest room, downstairs, or outside."

She nodded tearfully.

A small part of me felt bad for treating her so harshly but the rational part of me knew she deserved it.

I walked past her into my bedroom.

"Can we talk about it a different time?" she asked, her voice full of hope.

"I don't know, Cass," I answered truthfully.

"Okay."

I closed the door.

You have no reason to feel bad about this, Dakota.

I walked into the bathroom, eager to finally get my ass into a shower.

While I waited for the water to heat up, I poured myself some whiskey from the brand-new bottle Jace had given me as a best man gift.

I should have busted him upside the head with the bottle.

I turned up my glass, the warm drink burning the whole way down.

The burning means you're too alert. Better have another.

I poured another, chugging it all the way back before stripping down to get in the shower. The water was scalding hot, just the way I prefer it.

Just like the hot tub at the cabin.

The thought of the hot tub made me think of Lena.

Her dripping, curvy body leaned back against the side of the tub, her wet tank top melted against her skin, her body trembling as she came for me.

My cock grew harder and harder the more I thought about it.

I shouldn't be thinking of her like this. I had already made the decision that we would forget it ever happened, but as I replayed it all in my head, my balls started to ache at the thought of her. Before I realized what I was doing, I started stroking myself. Irritation overcame me as I fisted my dick, the grip nowhere near as amazing as her tight pussy.

Or her skillful mouth.

"Fuck, that mouth…" I moaned, jacking myself faster.

Her tonsils tightening around me…

With a jolt, I erupted, covering Cassie's expensive shampoo and conditioner bottles with a thick ribbon of cum. "Fuck!"

You have got to let this go. It was an incredibly vulnerable time and neither of us were thinkin' straight.

"It would never have happened under normal circumstances," I reminded myself.

And it will never happen again.

Jolene

The smell of bacon filled my nostrils.

Jace is cookin' breakfast?

I opened my eyes, panicking for a moment as I took in my surroundings. The events of the last few days came flooding back to me.

The wedding, the cabin, the snow, Dakota...

"I need to check on Dakota," I muttered to myself. Grabbing my phone off the nightstand, I unplugged the fluorescent orange charger.

Seven missed calls from Jace, three texts from him, and one picture message from Cassie.

What could she possibly be sending me pictures of?

I tapped the notification, and my screen lit up with a picture of a shirtless Dakota sleeping peacefully in their bed. The angle of the picture made it clear that she was in bed next to him. She had captioned the picture, "Can we make up, too?"

Seems like he got over her boning his bestie pretty quickly.

Disgusted, I put my phone back on the nightstand.

No point in texting him. She seems to have him covered.

Annoyed for reasons that I couldn't pin down, I climbed out of bed. "That explains what 'and, yeah' means," I grumbled to myself.

I slid my feet in my slippers and shuffled down the stairs.

The smell of breakfast grew stronger as I reached the bottom. Unsurprisingly, I found mama at the stove and daddy sitting at the kitchen table.

"Good mornin', Lee Lee!" he greeted me cheerfully as he took a sip of coffee.

"Mornin'." I gave him a one-armed hug.

"How'd you sleep, punkin'?" Mama asked as she poured me a cup of coffee.

"Like a rock," I admitted. Mama started beaming. "I'm so glad. I'm making omelets before your daddy goes out to feed the animals. Want one?"

I didn't but I knew it would worry her if I declined. "Yes, ma'am, thank you." I sat down next to my daddy, picking up the newspaper he had discarded on the table.

"Any interesting happenings in town?" I asked as I unfolded it.

Besides my own.

"The Roberts' boy got arrested again for drivin' drunk. His mugshot is on page three."

They may as well just keep him at the jail house. He gets arrested twice a month.

"His mama is so fed up with him. She was in the bank last week talkin' about it," I informed him. From the stove, Mama shook her head. "Arlene is so sweet. I hate it for her."

I nodded in agreement.

The mention of work reminded me I didn't have my car.

Dak said he would take me to get it this weekend, but he will probably be with Cassie…

"Hey, Dad, can you recommend a good towing company? Or a hauling company? I want to get my car brought back from the mountains."

"I thought Dak was gonna take you back this weekend?" Mama interjected.

Lord, forgive me for this lie I'm about to tell.

"He thinks he's gonna have to work," I fibbed.

"I'll call Jim over at Miles Towing and Recovery and get it here today," Dad promised.

Daddy for the win, as always.

"Thanks, Dad."

Mama sat a plate down in front of each of us. "Y'all, eat up. Lee, Jace's mama called here last night."

I nearly choked on my coffee. "What did she say?" I sputtered. She patted me on the back. "She just wanted to check on you. She said she had tried to call you a few times."

I didn't even check my missed calls yesterday when I cut my phone on.

"I have had my phone off," I explained. "I just didn't want to relive it over and over again."

Mama nodded sympathetically. "I understand, honey. She said she would check in on you later."

"Lee, did I tell you Milkshake had her calf?" My daddy deliberately changed the subject.

Thanks, Dad.

"No, sir! I want to see it when we are done eatin'!"

He smiled. He had never admitted it, but I knew he enjoyed that I loved our animals as much as he did.

"You have to put clothes on first because it's cold, but we can go after that."

Smiling, I took a bite of my omelet.

I've missed my mama's cookin'.

Eating at that farmer's speed, Dad finished before me. "I'm gonna go call Jim at Miles. Go change when you finish, and we will go see Milkshake."

With a mouthful of bacon, I gave him a thumbs up.

Cassie may have Jace and Dakota, but I've got a baby cow.

Dakota

Dedric popped his head into my office. "Check off inspection is done, Lieu. One of the air packs needed a new cylinder but I replaced it."

I looked up from my paperwork. "Good work, Rook. Make sure you fill out a report and date it."

"Yes, sir." He left the doorway.

It's good to be back at work.

I checked my phone for the fifteenth time.

Nothin'.

I had spent the afternoon catching up on paperwork and trying to decipher texts from Lena. Unlocking the phone, I opened our text feed. After rereading them yet again, I still couldn't figure out her tone.

My list of obligations? The fuck does she even mean by that?

"I was kinda excited to take her to get it," I mumbled to myself.

"You talkin' to yourself, Lieu?" Zeke teased.

"Reckon I was," I admitted. "What's up, bud?"

"I was just checkin' in on you." He shuffled his feet awkwardly. "I know all of this has been tough."

Even tougher when you can't decode someone's texts.

"It's…interesting. Cassie is moving her stuff all the way out today."

He looked surprised. "Damn, brother. No chance of reconciling?"

I shook my head firmly. "Not a one."

He nodded sympathetically. "Can't say I blame you. Too many out there to stay with one you can't trust."

I looked down at my phone.

Or one that sends confusing ass text messages.

The station bell rang, and we both paused for the radio transmission.

"Battalion 1, Engine 11…"

I jumped up from my desk.

"Respond to 505 Landon Lake Circle for a possible structure fire. Caller advised smoke coming from front windows."

The five of us dressed quickly. "Ben, put us en route!" He keyed up his lapel mic.

As we hauled ass out of the bay, Zeke switched on the Q siren. Turning to face the back, I began calling out assignments. "Ben, you're on the nozzle. Rook, you catch the hydrant, Zeke, Carter, y'all are with me on the search team. Everybody is goin' home, repeat it."

"Everybody is goin' home," they repeated in unison.

Zeke pulled the apparatus into a smoky neighborhood. I grabbed the truck's radio mic, ready to alert dispatch as I scanned the numerics. "This is 501…503…505, there it is!"

I keyed up the mic. "Battalion 1, Engine 11 on scene, working structure fire with smoke showing, Battalion 1 establishing command." My team and I piled out of the truck.

The neighbors had gathered in the front yard. "Anyone know of any occupants?" I asked. A big, burly man spoke up, "The man and woman are both at work, but they have two dogs."

"Zeke, Carter, let's set up or an interior attack, possible pets inside, go!" I barked. Putting on my air mask, I double checked my PASS alarm. "Let's go, y'all."

I fuckin' love this job.

Jolene

"What are you gonna name her?" my dad asked me as I cradled the adorable calf.

"She's a week old! Mama hasn't already named her?"

He continued raking the hay out in Milkshake's pen. "No, ma'am, Charlie Girl wanted to leave it up to you. She knows how much you love namin' 'em."

I do love namin' my babies.

"What about…," I began. "Milkdud."

"Milkdud?"

"Yes, sir," I proclaimed proudly.

"I like it. It suits her."

I cradled the baby cow's head. "Welcome to the family, Milkdud."

Across the pen, I caught my daddy smiling. "Why're you lookin' like the cat that caught the canary?" I teased him. Putting down the rake, he walked over to me and Milkdud.

"I'm just glad you're home, Lee Lee," he spoke softly. "I wish it wasn't under these circumstances but I worry about you when you're not here."

Bless his heart.

"I know you do…but you know that whether I'm here, at Jace's, or in my own place, I'm always gonna come home."

He nodded. "I know it, but a dad is always gonna worry unless he has his eyes on you."

"Did you worry about me when I was at Jace's?" I asked curiously.

He laughed, the noise startling poor Milkdud.

"I've been worried for more than thirty years. Ever since that doctor handed me that little pink blanket. Nothin' was the same after that."

You had already been a daddy five years at that point…

"You already had Cruise when I was born," I pointed out. "It wasn't like you were new at it."

"Cruise is a boy, though. I knew he would be rough and tough. You were tiny and fragile. I was worried the world would eat you alive."

Kinda offensive that you labeled me as weak from the jump, Pops.

When I didn't respond, he continued. "I was wrong, though. You ate the world alive. You became hardheaded, determined, and brave. You grew into a force to be reckoned with… but at the end of the day, you're my baby and I'm always gonna wanna fix anything that hurts you."

The world doesn't deserve my daddy.

I slid Milkdud's head out of my lap and stood up. "You're the best dad in the world and Cruise and I are lucky to have you." I gave him a big hug.

He cleared his throat awkwardly. "Enough of all this. Grab that basket. Go get those eggs gathered and take 'em to your mama."

I smiled. "Yes, sir."

Pulling my phone from my back pocket, I checked my texts while I walked to the chicken coop.

Two missed calls from Jace, a Facebook notification, and a text from Dakota.

I tapped the notification eagerly.

The plan was to go this weekend but with the chance of being around Cassie? No, thanks.

I typed a quick response and pressed send.

●●●○○ Verizon LTE   2:59 PM   ✻ 86% ▬▬

‹ Messages   **Dak**   Details

Good mornin' Lena Loo!
Just checkin' on you! I'm
at HQ if you need me!

Mornin. I'm ok thanks.
Mr. Jim at Miles Towing
is goin to the cabin today
to get my car so you can
take that off the list of
obligations.

Obligations? I didn't mind
doing it.. I thought the
plan was to go this
weekend?

It's handled. Thanks,
though. Stay safe today.

iMessage

Before sliding my phone back in my pocket, I opened Cassie's picture message again. Dak looked so peaceful, sleeping just the way he was sleeping next to me in the mountains.

Maybe it's an old picture.

Dipping into my crazy reservoir, I remembered there was a way to check the metadata of a picture if you have an iPhone.

I saved the picture she sent me to my phone's camera roll.

Let's see if I can remember how to do this.

I tapped the information button in the center of the options at the bottom of the phone then scrolled down to the metadata. Sure enough, it told me what type of phone the picture was taken on, the picture settings that were used, the time the picture was taken, and of course, the date it was taken.

And it was taken last night after he left my house.

Anger unfurled in the pit of my stomach.

She is his fiancé and you're being a fuckin' nutjob about this.

I knew I was being unreasonable, but it didn't stop my anger from intensifying with every step I took.

I guess she's able to convince a man to do anything so long as she doesn't have clothes on... the bad part is, the men are just as weak as she is.

Dakota

"Good work, y'all. Let's get the truck back in service."

Nothin' like a good workin' structure fire to get the blood punmpin'.

I pulled the hose off.

"Lieutenant, can I see you in my office?" Chief Hennessy called out into the bay.

"Comin', Chief," I called back. "Y'all keep goin', I'll be right back."

I walked into the station to find the Chief standing at the kitchen counter. "Let's go to my office, DK." He gestured for me to follow him.

Oh, lawd, I'm about to catch hell for the window ordeal.

I followed him into his office, shutting the door behind me.

"Have a seat."

I sat in the chair across from his desk. "So, I've been thinkin' it over and in regard to Jace switchin' to this shift," he began, "I've decided that I have faith that y'all can conduct yourselves to the standards we have set for this department."

I nodded. "Yes, sir."

"It was already the plan to move him because we need a sixth guy so we will be stacked if we need a second apparatus."

"Whatever you think is best, Chief. I know I speak for myself and Jace when I say that our personal issues won't penetrate these walls."

He nodded. "I trust they won't. That's all I needed," he dismissed me. "Good work today."

I stood up. "'Preciate it, Chief."

Zeke met me in the kitchen. "Truck is back in service, Lieu."

"Fantastic. Rally the guys, would ya? I have an announcement."

"Will do." He headed back out into the bay.

May as well nip this shit in the bud before it starts.

Ten minutes later, the four of them were standing in my office waiting to hear what I had to say.

"Chief pulled me in earlier and let me know that Reynolds is still goin' to be transferrin' over to our shift."

Their eyes widened.

"With that bein' said, I don't want anyone stating the obvious. I don't want any mention of everything that is goin' on. None of it breeches these walls. Understood?"

They all agreed.

"I know it will seem awkward at first," I continued. "But we all have a job to do. Jace is our brother inside of the walls, mine included."

More agreeing.

"Aight, that's it. Y'all go eat somethin' and rest up for the next one."

They hurried out of my office. With a sigh, I picked up my phone from my desk. The home screen showed a text from Lena.

It's handled, thanks? The fuck? What's with the cold shoulder?

Ignoring her brush off, I sent her another message before checking my other texts. I had one from my daddy, one from my neighbor up the road, and two from Cassie.

Why the fuck are you texting me?

Irritated, I opened them, completely unsurprised to see that one of them was a naked picture of herself.

Why does she think she can sexualize her way out of this?

My phone vibrated in my hand. My stomach dipped when I realized it was a text from Lena.

I'm sorry, what?

Rage turned over in my gut.

That didn't take long.

I wanted to ask her if she had lost her damn mind. I wanted to flip my desk the fuck over. I wanted to go to her house and talk some sense into her, but deep down, I knew it was her life, and she was smart enough to make her own decisions.

No matter how completely fuckin' stupid the decisions are.

I couldn't think of a supportive response, so I decided not to reply at all.

After putting my phone in the top drawer, I stood up from my desk chair.

Time to go take out every bit of this goddamn frustration in the weight room.

Jolene

I can't believe I sent that text.

I knew I shouldn't have but I was still so irritated from Cassie's dumbass picture message that I sent it without thinking.

Talkin' to Jace was a diabolical text to send, knowing the only thing you said to Jace was that he needed to stop callin' you.

I checked my home screen for a response from Dak, disappointed to find there was nothing there. I tapped our text feed.

He read it thirteen minutes ago…

"He better not be judging me. A text is nothin' compared to sleepin' with someone," I said to myself.

I unbraided my hair, lettin' it fall in loose waves.

My mama stuck her head in my room. "Your car is here, honey!"

Thank goodness.

"Great, thanks, Mama!"

Time to do a little…investigating.

Grabbing my keys and my purse, I ran down the stairs, taking them two at a time.

"I'll be back, Mama!" I called out, grabbing my boots on the way out the front door.

"Where you headed, Shug?" My daddy questioned from around the side of the porch.

I didn't even see him standin' there.

He was painting my mama's rocking chairs, the man unable to let his hands ever rest.

I walked over to where he was working. "I'm gonna go by the bank, Dad," I lied. "Just gonna go say hey to everybody. I'm goin' stir crazy."

He slowly dragged his brush along the arm rail. "I understand."

"Thanks for gettin' my car home for me! I'll be back soon." I kissed the top of his old, faded Georgia Bulldogs hat.

I climbed in my car before he could ask any more questions, the scent of Jace's cologne smacking me in the face.

Why the fuck does my car smell like him?

I pulled out of my driveway with one destination in mind: Dakota's house.

You are officially batshit crazy.

Cranking the music up to drown out my voice of reason, I drove straight to Dakota's street.

You're gonna have to open the garage door to even see if she's there, Jolene.

When my voice of reason starts using my government name, I know I've gone too far, but I lifted my center console, anyways. With the compartment opened, I fumbled around inside, feeling around for the garage door opener he had given me years ago.

The rumble strips vibrated underneath my tires.

Keep your eyes on the road, bitch.

While cussing myself mentally for having a cluttered car, I finally located the device. Pulling up into his driveway, I pressed the button to open his garage. Within seconds, the door began to lift, revealing a certain black Ford Escape.

She's here.

I pressed the button again to close the door before putting my car in reverse.

You are officially insane.

Leaving his street, I drove towards town, unsure of where I was actually going from here. I passed by the church where my world had stopped turning.

How does that feel like it happened five minutes ago and five weeks ago, all at the same damn time.

I was still supposed to be on my honeymoon, living in perfectly matched newlywedded bliss and somehow, I'm riding around stalking my former best friend who was sleeping with my fiancé because I'm pissed that she's sleeping with her own fiancé who is my former fiancé's best friend.

If you listen reeeeeaally closely, you'll hear "Jerry! Jerry! Jerry!"

I turned into the old Save- A- Lot parking lot to give myself a minute. I could feel myself getting worked up and the way my anxiety is set up…

I looked around the car for five things I could touch, smell, and feel.

Steering wheel… air freshener… satin hair scrunchie on the rearview… Jace's suitcase…

Jace's suitcase.

That's why it smells like his cologne in here.

In all the chaos, I had forgotten that he had it in here so we could leave straight for the cabin.

Before I could talk myself out of it, I crept out of the parking lot. I didn't want to see him, but I didn't want his stuff anywhere near me.

I cruised down the road I had driven many, many times before eventually turning onto the pathway that led to the house that I once considered my own. Tears threatened when I pulled into my spot as I took in the way that nothing outside of the house had changed. The rocking chairs were situated the way I had put them; the little Christmas trees were still on the porch. The wreath I had made at a local boutique still hung on the door, proudly bearing the name I was so excited to take. As I stared at the house that I had found and picked out, I allowed myself a few minutes to grieve.

I grieved for the choices I didn't get to make, and the ones I had made far too wrong.

I grieved for the future I had planned to a T, and the one I couldn't plan now at all.

I grieved for the feeling of knowing I was loved and for the worry I'd never really felt it at all.

I grieved for the trust I'd given so freely and for the fear that I'd never trust again.

I grieved for my best friend and the lifetime we'd spent together and for the lifetime we would now spend apart.

I grieved for my high school sweetheart and the time we had spent together and for the time we would never have again.

I grieved for the girl that I had grown up to be and for the girl I'm now forced to become.

Tears splashed at my thighs as I gave into the pain.

As I pulled it together, I pulled out my phone, my fingers shakily typing out a text.

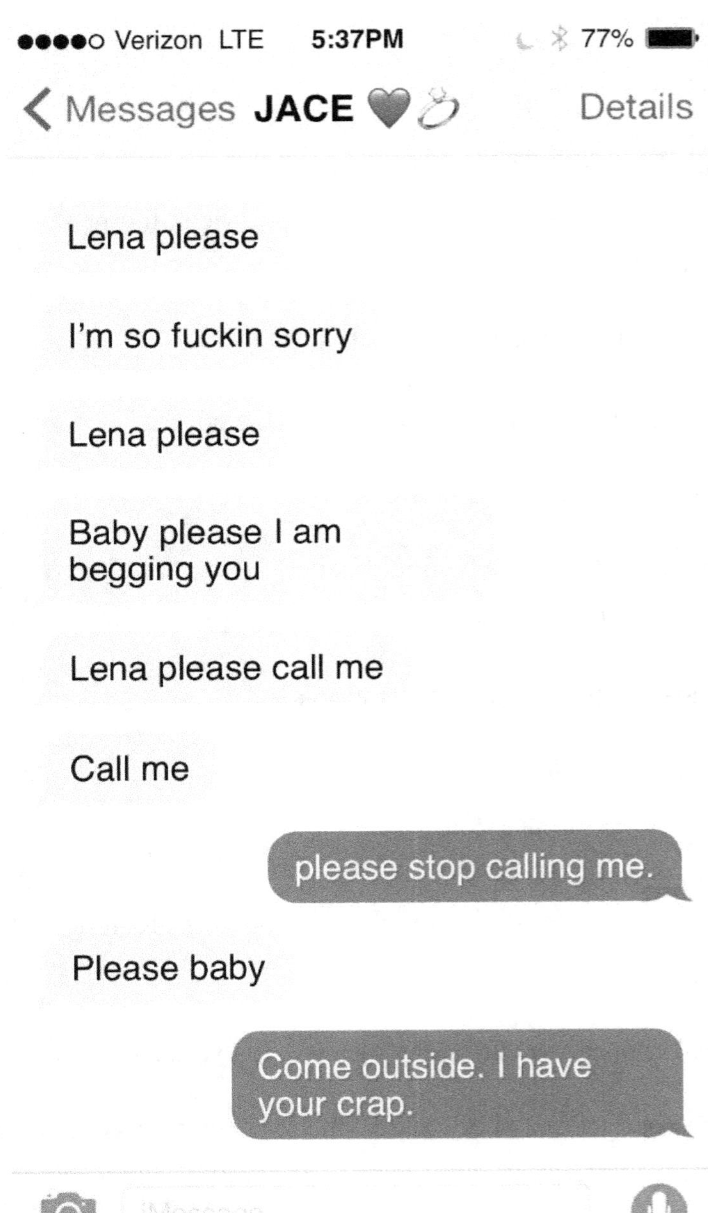

A split second later, the front door opened, and my ex-fiancé walked out. I grabbed his bag from the back seat before climbing out of the car.

"Hey, Lenie," he spoke softly.

He looked like shit. He looked like he hadn't slept in days and like there wasn't a razor left in the house. For a weak moment, my heart went out to him.

"I have your bag." I held it out to him.

He took it from me and sat it on the porch step.

"I figured you had thrown it away."

I leaned against my car. "I should have." He ran his fingers through his unruly wild, unwashed hair. "I wouldn't have blamed you."

His lying eyes had the audacity to look sad.

I don't want to be here.

"I'm gonna go."

He grabbed my arm, and I pulled away, his touch feeling as if it had burned me.

"Please, Lena, can we talk?" he pleaded, his voice wavering.

Blinking back tears, I shook my head. "Nothin' you say is goin' to make a difference.
Nothin' changes reality."

Getting in my car, I pulled away without a backwards glance.

A part of me felt relieved.

I knew my worth and wouldn't allow myself to settle for less, but the other half of me was disappointed that Dakota didn't value himself the same way.

Dakota

"What's up, JR?" I overheard Zeke say.

Jace is here.

Reluctantly, I stood up from my desk, determined to fulfil my role as Lieutenant without my personal feelings coming into play.

I walked into the station's living room. Ben and Dedric were playing football on the PlayStation; Carter and Zeke were propped up at the kitchen island, deep in conversation with Jace. He stopped mid-sentence when he saw me.

"Lieutenant." He nodded respectfully. I nodded back. "Good afternoon. I have some paperwork ready for you whenever you're ready. No rush, take your time."

"Yes, sir." He went back to talking.

He has never once called me Lieutenant as a serious title. I've always been DK.

After grabbing a bottle of water, I went back to my office. With a shaky breath, I checked my phone, praying for a text message from Lena. Disappointment flooded my veins when I saw that she hadn't texted me. Cassie had, of course, but I deleted those texts without even reading them.

From behind me, knuckles tapped against the doorframe.

"Busy?" Jace asked quietly. I sat my phone down but couldn't be bothered to turn around.

"Not at all. Come on in."

He walked cautiously into my office, shutting the door behind him. He sat down awkwardly across from my desk, clearly uncomfortable and unsure of what to say.

How many times have we sat in here just shootin' the shit and fuckin' off.

For the first time since all of this happened, the sadness felt stronger than the anger. Jace and I had been friends for two decades. He's been there for every milestone, hard moment, and everything in between.

And I'm gonna miss my fuckin' buddy.

The lump in my throat came out of nowhere but I was determined to choke it down.

"Sorry, I'm late. Lena came by the house," he explained.

Okay, we are back to anger.

I did my best to keep my tone professional. "It's no problem. You weren't on a time clock. I just need you to sign your transfer paperwork." I slid a piece of paper across the desk. Picking it up, he looked it over, knowing damn well what the fuck it said already.

"Gotta pen?" he asked.

No, dumbass, I like to chisel all my paperwork in stone.

I grabbed a pen from the jar on my desk and tossed it to him. He signed the paper with a flourish and slid it back across my desk.

"'Preciate it. Everything else will remain the same. Same locker, bunk, same everything. The only change is you work the opposite shift now, starting tomorrow."

He nodded.

"Any questions?" I asked as I signed my own name on the form.

"Just one," he began. "Are we gonna be able to do this without killin' each other?

His straightforwardness caught me off guard. I cleared my throat.

"In this building, you are a brother. I've got your back no matter what and I hope you've got mine. No part of our personal problems will exist here. There will be no mention of it. We will come here, do the job that we vowed to do for this community, and go home."

He nodded in agreement. "If there's nothing else, Lieutenant, I'm gonna head out. I'll see you tomorrow."

We both stood. He extended his hand, and I shook it, doing my damndest to live up to the title the Chief thought I deserved.

And I thought the hardest part of this job would be the whole goin' inside a burnin' building thing.

Jolene

"We've been prayin' for you, Doll Baby!" Mrs. Cheryl told me with a head tilt and a sympathetic smile. "How are you holdin' up?"

I was already regretting my decision to stop by the bank, but I was trying to weasel my way out of the guilt of lying to my daddy and since the bank was open until 8PM today, I couldn't resist stopping.

I'm just takin' it one day at a time," I told her.

Definitely stole that line from Dakota.

She pursed her lips together in disapproval. "We are all so disappointed in Jace," she mused. "We weren't all that surprised about Cassie, though."

What? Why?

Before I could ask, she continued. "Her mama was always fast and loose, too, flauntin' her fanny at any man that looked at it."

Oh, Lord bless.

I had heard plenty of stories about Cassie's mama over the years, about how she hid her promiscuity behind her church desk.

Oh, the fuckin' irony.

"Lena? Is that you?" Big Jake called from his office.

"Yes, sir, it's me," I hollered back.

"Come on in here, Shug."

Saved by the boss man.

"Sorry, Mrs. Cheryl," I apologized. "I'll be back."

Feeling relieved, I walked into Dakota's daddy's office.

He greeted me with a hug… something he's always done but never at work.

"How you holdin' up, Shug?" he asked me, holding me at arm's length.

I felt myself tearing up. Big Jake was like a second daddy to me, but not so much that I knew he would lose sleep over it like my real daddy.

"I'm strugglin', Mr. Clayton," I admitted as much to myself as I was to him.

"No, ma'am, no formalities," he scolded gently. "You're not at work right now."

"Yes, sir."

He gestured for me to sit down. "How's Dak holdin' up?" he asked as he handed me a bottle of water.

"He's back at work today," I began. "Cassie is still at his house."

"She what?" His face clouded up with anger.

I explained what I knew, leaving out the part about Cassie's little picture message.

"I would have thought his standards were higher than that," he stated truthfully.

"Love is a bitch," I reminded him. "Dak loved, or I guess loves, her with all his heart."

The words tasted bitter in my mouth. I took a sip of water.

"Maybe so, but she clearly doesn't reciprocate it," he pointed out, the statement dripping with disappointment.

He's always loved me and Cassie like we are the daughters he never had.

"You won't catch me arguing that."

He sat back in his expensive chair. "I'm askin' as someone that loves you like a daughter, not as your boss," he prefaced. "Where do you see thing landing with Jace?"

I felt the damned tears brewing again. "It's over for me," I told him honestly. "I went to his house earlier to give him a bag of his stuff that he had in my car for the honeymoon, and it made me sick to even look at him." I swallowed hard. "I don't know for sure, but I think I might have been able to work through it, to work it out with him, if it had been anybody else but Cassie."

Noticing the tear sliding down my cheek, he passed me the handkerchief from his front pocket.

"It's a different level of betrayal," he spoke softly. "Dak doesn't know this… but when he was little, his mama cheated on me with a friend of mine."

My mouth dropped open in horror.

"It was before the bank opened," he went on, "I was still workin' at the fire department – it was before the accident – but she was foolin' around with one of the guys that worked the day shift when I was on nights."

Big Jake had been a firefighter when Dakota was little. An injury had taken him off the job and Clayton Community Bank was born.

I was at a loss for words. "I'm so sorry. I had no idea."

He rubbed his stubbly chin. "Not many do," he confided. "I kept it under wraps because Dak was friends with Gentry's son at school."

This town is just full of shitty people.

"Waylon Gentry?"

He nodded. "Dakota and Jacob were good buddies. Played rec ball together, they were in the same class at school, and they did FFA together," he spoke as if the nearly twenty-five-year-old memory pained him. "His mama was already horrible to him. Never there, ya know… so, I kept my mouth shut about it, so she wasn't able to ruin something else."

My heart went out to him. We were just two blind fools, sittin' here, puttin' our faith in the wrong people.

"I tell you that for one reason, Lee Lee," he sat straight up in his chair. "If you are forced to forgive someone enough times, you will eventually start to hate them."

What does that mean?

"What I mean is…," he continued as if he were reading my mind. "Every time you forgive them, you lose a piece of yourself until you eventually become someone you don't even recognize… and you will resent them for causing it."

His words danced around in my mind.

"Forgive that man, Jolene, for your own sake… but do not forget. When someone shows you who they are – believe them."

I took a long sip of water.

"Yes, sir."

He went back to his computer. "Take all the time off you need, honey. Your job is here when you're ready."

"Thanks, Big Jake."

I walked out of his office with more mental clarity than I'd had in in months.

Long before this happened.

Jace had done things that required my forgiveness long before now. He would be mean to me if I spoke up about something I wanted to do differently in our relationship, tear me down mentally by attacking my insecurities when we would fight, he would bring his mama into our arguments then stand by while she berated me… I had forgiven a lot of things that I hadn't been okay with because I loved him.

After talking to Big Jake, I realized that with every single thing I overlooked that I wasn't okay with, I gave up a small piece of myself.

That's why I have no interest in forgiving him. I've given all I have to give.

I quickly walked back across the bank lobby, eager to get out to my car before I was stopped by someone else.

These damn holiday hours we do this time of year have this place entirely too busy for this time of day.

"Lena!" a familiar voice rang out.

Fuckkkk me.

At the teller counter, in all her overly made-up glory, was Jace's mama.

Fuck, fuck FUCK!

She embraced me with fake sincerity. "Sweet Lena, how are you, honey?" she asked, her eyes filling with tears.

Oh, so we are puttin' on a show.

"I'm doin' good," I answered calmly. "How are you, Mrs. Linda?"

"I am heartbroken!" she wailed, pulling me into her cigarette and Chanel No. 5 scented chest.

You are in your place of employment, Lena. Mind your manners.

"I'm sorry to hear that." I pulled away from her. "It will all be okay."

The fact that I'm having to stand here and comfort this narcissistic bitch so that she doesn't make a scene...

"I can't wait to hear that you and Jace have patched things up!" she practically shouted.

"That won't be happening, Mrs. Linda," I spoke gently.

She put her hand to her chest in mock horror. "Jolene, you have to be reasonable!" she quietly scolded. "Boys will be boys!"

Bitch, I know you fuckin' lyin'...

I forgot where I was. I forgot all my home trainin'.

"I think what you mean to say," I began, "is that pieces of shit will be pieces of shit."

"Jolene!" she chastised me. "That is unnecessary!"

"Do not tell me what is unnecessary! The whole time I was with that man, I was prayin' that he would rise above his raising because Lord knows, if you had as many stickin' out of you as you've had stuck in you, you'd be a primped-up porcupine! I guess the apple truly doesn't fall far from the tree that everyone gets to climb, now does it?"

Her mouth hung open in genuine horror and dismay.

"You and Jace are both like a doorknob," I continued. "Everybody gets a turn! Now, I have spent more than enough of my precious time entertaining you. Have the evening that you deserve."

With a jaunty wave to my friends behind the counter, I walked out the front door.

Dakota

"Awesome job, y'all. Go on back to bed. I'll get her back in service," I gestured to the engine.

"I'll help, Lieu," Dedric volunteered.

"Thanks, Rook."

We worked in exhausted silence to get the truck back in service.

We were nearly finished when I caught him yawning. "Go back to bed, D, I'll get the rest."

"Thanks, Lieutenant."

"You did a great job today. Keep up the good work," I told him.

He fist bumped me. "Learned from the best. G'night, buddy."

"Goodnight."

I walked around the apparatus, inspecting her to make sure she was locked and loaded for when the next tone dropped.

Three structure fires in one day is a sure sign that it's space heater season.

I hung up the used hoses so they could dry.

Finally. She's ready to go again.

Walking across the bay, I glanced up at the analog clock.

Only an hour and a half left. Please, Lord, keep it calm.

I stepped into my office.

"Too late to go back to sleep. May as well organize this crap," I groaned, staring at my desk. I gathered the stacks of paperwork, making sure they were in correct order, and put them in the file cabinet.

Finishing quicker than I thought I would, I pulled my phone from my desk drawer.

No texts from Lena, two video messages from Cassie, and two missed calls from my dad.

She and Jace must have made up. Nothin' but the cold shoulder or radio silence all day.

Jace's words replayed in my mind.

"Lena came by the house."

"That's why she wanted her car!" I shouted out into my dimly lit office.

Bile rose in my throat.

Why would she stay with him knowin' the type of person he is?

I made a plan to go to her house to talk some sense into her the second that my shift ended.

"Burnin' the midnight… or 5AM oil?" Chief Hennessy interrupted my thoughts.

"I figured I'd get these reports finished and filed," I lied. "Why are you awake?"

He leaned against my doorframe. "Worried about my Lieutenant."

"I'm good, Chief."

"Quit all that lyin'."

I sighed. "I just… I realized today that I've lost someone that was like a brother to me… and it stings a little."

"Everyone in your life is either a blessin' or a lesson."

"That's what I've heard."

"It'll get better, Dakota. Not tomorrow, probably not next week, maybe not even next month… but it will get better. One day at a time."

"Yes, sir. Thanks, Chief."

We walked out of the office, leaving me to my own devices. One of which I picked up and used to type a text out to Lena. I read it and reread it, and before I could talk myself out of it, I pressed send.

●●●○○ Verizon LTE   5:02 AM   60%

‹ Messages   Loo   Details

Obligations? I didn't mind doing it.. I thought the plan was to go this weekend?

It's handled. Thanks, though. Stay safe today.

What are you up to?

Talkin to jace

Nights like tonight REALLY make me wish that me, you and a bottle of Jack Daniels were back in the hot tub.

iMessage

This will either be the lesson or the blessin'.

Jolene

I stared at Dakota's text on my phone screen.

Me, him and the whiskey in the hot tub… where's his fiancé in this scenario? Passin' out towels?

Pissed off, I locked my phone and sat it on the nightstand.

I wanted to text him back but knowing that he was about to go home to Cassie was stopping me.

I'm sure she would jump at the chance to get naked, especially in the hot tub.

Grabbing my Roku remote, I switched on my tv. With Christmas only a little over a week away, it would be easy to find a good movie to watch. After a minute of scrolling, I settled on Home Alone 2: Lost in New York.

A classic.

Kevin was just starting to explore Duncan's Toy Chest when my phone started to vibrate. Picking it up, I read the name on the screen.

Dakota.

Curiosity got the best of me.

"Hello?"

"Are you awake?"

"Obviously."

Silence…

"You didn't answer my text."

"Three's a crowd," I told him, trying to keep the bitterness out of my voice.

"What?"

"Nevermind, Dak."

"No, explain what you are ta– **riiiiiiiiingggg!** – fuck!"

Duty calls.

"Be safe."

"Talk later."

He hung up.

That was completely pointless.

Hearing from him and trying to play it cool made me feel exhausted. Like, can't hold my eyes open, gotta go to sleep now, exhausted.

Unfortunately, I couldn't go to sleep after hearing the tones drop until I knew all the guys were safe, back at the station. I opened the Follow 911 app on my phone.

"Battalion 1, engine 11 on scene."

Damn, must have been pretty close to headquarters.

"Battalion 1, Engine 11, be advised – working structure fire – heavy smoke showing."

"Battalion 1 – Command copies. Working structure fire – smoke showing."

Fuck…

The fear that overtakes my veins whenever I learn that Jace, Dakota, or any of the guys have a working structure fire has been there since Jace and Dakota started at Creek's Edge Fire Department, and it's only grown over time. Once I got to know the other guys on the team and their families, I started worrying about them all.

Okay, give me some radio traffic so I can breathe.

"Battalion 1 to Command, be advised 1211, 1302, 1317, starting primary search."

He's going in after someone.

"Battlation 1 – 1211 - Command copies."

"1211 to Command, fire showing on back side of first floor."

I watched Kevin roam with the pigeon lady, trying to convince myself I wasn't on pins and needles.

Honestly, I like the pigeon lady. She stays mindin' her birds and her business.

"Command, Battalion 1 – 1211 – be advised – primary search terminated. 1211 requesting coroner."

Oh no...

"Command to Battalion 1 – 1211 – coroner is en route."

I said a silent prayer for the family.

Suddenly my problems seemed very, very small.

Dakota

What. A. Fuckin'. Night.

I drove home with the radio off. The only noise in the cab was from the bag on the window.

This might be a record night.

Turning in my driveway, I mashed the button on my sun visor. Cassie's car was still parked inside my garage, her knowing damn well she is supposed to be out of my fucking house.

I'm done playin' fuckin' nice.

I flung open the door, the force sending it slamming into my kitchen wall.

"Cassie!" I hollered. "Where the fuck are you at?!"

She came sauntering out of the living room, wearing a dress that was so small, it barely qualified as clothing.

"Good mornin', how was work?" she asked as if everything was normal.

"Get out of my house."

"What?" She looked confused.

"Get the fuck out of my house!" I hollered.

"What is wrong with you!?" she cried out.

"You! You are what the fuck is wrong with me!" I screamed. "How can you have the balls to still be sittin' your ass up in my house!?

"Where do you expect me to go, Dak?!" she shot back. "I don't have anyone!"

"Go to a hotel. Go to Jace's. Go to HELL! I don't give a fuck. Just get the fuck out of my house."

She started to cry. "Why can't you just forgive me?"

"Because you are not fuckin' sorry! You are sorry you got CAUGHT! That's it!"

"That's not true!" she protested.

"Your best friend's fiancé on their wedding day in the church office! Between you and your mama, that desk has some miles on it!"

"Oh, so you're goin' low," she pointed out.

"Cassie, YOU went low! The fuck! That was my best fuckin' friend since I was a goddamn kid!"

Reign it in, Dak, reign it in...

"If you will just listen to me, I -," she began.

"I do not care. I don't care. Get out of my house. Now." I stomped up the stairs. "If you are still here when I wake up, I'm callin' the damn law!"

I slammed my bedroom door.

Why the fuck can't people just do what they're supposed to do! Don't rail people that aren't yours to rail. Don't plug space heaters into anything besides the actual goddamn outlet. Don't leave candles burnin' while you go to fuckin' sleep!

I dragged myself into the shower, the smell of stale smoke filling the air as the scalding water heated my bare skin.

This wasn't the first time me and the guys had gotten to the scene a little too late. It wasn't the first time we had pulled somebody out that was no longer with us. It wasn't the first time and wouldn't be the last, but it never got any easier.

This is when I need Lena's goofy ass here to call me a dumb fuck or to whack me with a pillow.

Vowing to call her when I got out, I scrubbed myself a little faster. When I was sure I was clean and didn't smell like the job, I switched off the water.

I dried off quickly before brushing my teeth, the last step before finally being ready for bed.

I'm sleepin' naked today. Fuck clothes.

Grabbing my phone off the nightstand, I crawled into bed. I dialed her number from memory, my anxiety growing as I waited for her to answer. As I was getting ready to hang up, a sleepy voice came on the line.

"Hello?"

"Good mornin', beautiful."

I heard her yawn. "Good mornin'."

"How'd you sleep?" I asked her.

"Not enough, but okay, I guess. I fell asleep waiting on y'all to go back in service."

She was listening to the scanner.

"We were out there awhile."

"I heard it was a rough call." I could hear the sympathy in her voice.

"It was," I admitted.

"I'm sorry."

I sighed. "These days never get easier, ya know? They were gone already before we got there... There was nothin' we could have done, but for some reason, none of us see it that way. This one was only about a mile and a half from headquarters over on Parrish

Street. We all kept saying, if we had walked outside, we would have smelled the smoke and went sooner," I rambled.

"You can't think like that, Dakota. None of y'all can. Even if you had gone outside and smelled smoke, It's December. People have fires in their fireplaces all over the city." She suddenly sounded wide awake.

"I know you're right," I admitted. "It's just hard to get past it when you have one job and you just… can't do it."

"Some things are just out of our control. If this last week has taught us anything, it's that."

She has a point.

"I know."

"Get some rest, Dak. Things will seem clearer when you wake up."

"When I got off this morning, Lena, I got home and I…I just wanted to talk to you. That's such a weird feeling to me. Not that I didn't always like talkin' to you, you've been one of my best friends for years, but like, I wanted to talk to you."

She sighed. "Put down the drink and go to sleep, bud."

The drink? What?

"I'm not drinking anything? You know I don't drink when I get off shift if there's been a fatality. That takes it from a social drink to a coping drink in my mind and you know I don't do that. I won't ever drink to cope with doing my job."

She already knows this.

"Okay. Get some rest, anyways. You have to work tonight."

"Lena, what's going on?"

"I'm tired. It's 7AM and I was up until after five. Goodnight."

What the FUCK?

She has always been grouchy when she wakes up but that seemed to be extreme, even for her.

A thought popped into my head that added to the wonder that already was this shitty ass day.

She's in bed with Jace.

I sat up in bed, my crazy amping up, deciding on whether or not to drive by their house. If her car was there, she had to be there, and I'd be able to see from the road.

The only thing that stopped me was the day ahead, and the knowledge that I needed to rest to be able to do my job safely.

The community deserves you well rested and capable and your team deserves you well rested and capable. If she's at his house, she has made her decision and it's her decision to make.

Jolene

I couldn't fall back asleep.

The sound of Dakota's voice as he described that part of the job was haunting me all the way to my core.

He needed a friend, Lena, and you rejected him.

I felt sick to my stomach.

But I don't understand why he decided to call me…

Jace never discussed this part of the job. He always said he left it at the door. I respected the way he chose to handle it and never pressed him to talk. I knew that Dakota would open up to Cassie, but he's never called and done it with me.

Part of me contemplated calling him back, to be there, to be his friend… but I decided against it.

I don't want to be the source of any issue between him and Cassie, especially since she knows what we were up to in the mountains.

The more I thought about the two of them, the more I didn't understand how mine and Dakota's friendship would survive it.

If he was able to look past it, that was one thing, but I wouldn't ever be able to.

I wouldn't ever want to be around her and she, understandably, wouldn't want him around me alone. No matter how I envisioned it, I couldn't see a possible way that our friendship would survive all of this, even though he and I hadn't done a damn thing wrong.

Fed up with my own thoughts, I jumped out of bed and pulled on a pair of leggings.

I'll go help Daddy with the animals. That should be more than enough to distract me.

After throwing on a hoodie I had stolen from Jace years ago, I pulled my hair into a messy bun.

I didn't smell breakfast, meaning Mama must have slept in, so I tiptoed quietly down the stairs. Daddy was sitting at the kitchen table, a half empty coffee mug nearby. When I walked in the kitchen, he looked up in surprise.

"Lee Lee, good mornin'… are you okay?" He looked worried.

Bless his heart.

"Good mornin', Daddy! I'm okay. I just wanted to help you out this mornin!"

Okay, don't oversell it, you dumb bitch.

"I don't believe that for a second, but I'll be glad to let you help."

I poured myself a cup of coffee. "Thanks."

He put down the morning paper. "Your Mama is at the hospital with Arlene Roberts. Her sister passed away in a housefire last night and one of Arlene's nephews is badly burned."

That would be the house on Parrish Street…

"I heard about that."

His brow furrowed. "Jace?"

I shook my head quickly. "No, sir. Dak. He called this mornin' and he was pretty shaken up about it." He folded up the paper before laying it on the table.

"I bet he was. Arlene told your Mama they left a candle burnin' and the cat wound up knockin' the curtain into it. From my understandin', it was pretty out of control by the time a neighbor called it in."

That's so damn sad.

I took a sip of my coffee. "I listened to the scanner for a bit. I didn't hear whose house it was, but I did hear Dakota call for the coroner."

He nodded. "Hopefully, you talked him through it. That mess will stay with you if you let it."

Well, Dad, I didn't because I am as confused as Ronnie Milsap with a Where's Waldo book.

"I didn't really know what to say," I admitted. "Jace never talked about it at all. He would tell me they had fatalities, but he wouldn't talk about it beyond that. He always said he left it at work."

"Some men aren't big talkers." He got up to pour himself more coffee.

"I guess I just didn't understand why Dakota called me."

He sat down, looking confused. "Why wouldn't he call you?"

"What do you mean?"

"You said you don't understand why he called you…why wouldn't he? Y'all have been friends since y'all were kids."

You're making me sound even more ridiculous.

"I know that… but he's never done it before."

"Things aren't like they used to be before," he pointed out.

"Cassie is still at his house, Daddy," my voice wavered. He noticed immediately.

He put down his cup and focused on me. "Did you ask him if he decided to stay with her?"

"No, sir."

"Why not?"

Why haven't I just asked him?

"I guess because I'm not sure if it's my business. I guess I feel like if he wanted me to know then he would have told me."

He blew on his black coffee. "If he wanted you to know, he would make sure you know."

That's…what I just said.

"I think so, too. Dakota has always been up front about everything with everybody."

He nodded. "So, if he hasn't told you, why do you think they're back together?"

This is so a conversation for Mama.

"Cassie sent me a picture of them in bed."

His eyes widened and he cleared his throat.

"She shouldn't have done that. That's just distasteful."

Oh fuck, he's thinking it was something sexual.

I didn't know how to explain that it wasn't a full-on sexual picture, but I also didn't know how to explain how I knew the angle she was at to take the picture because I've woken up next to him the same way.

Can we just go feed the animals?

"I'll call him later to check on him, Dad. Ready to go start the day?"

Dakota

"IF I HAD TWOOOO DOZEN ROSES…"

My alarm ripped me out of a deep sleep.

Right in the middle of a damn good dream.

I checked the time.

3:30PM.

I didn't have to be at work until 6PM but I loved being able to shower and doddle around before going in, so I always set my alarm a little early.

But first, coffee…

I threw on a pair of gray sweatpants before heading downstairs, praying to the Lord above that Cassie had taken the hint and left.

Downstairs was empty, all traces of her existence no longer visible to the naked eye.

Hallelujah!

After starting the Keurig, I peeked into the garage. The Ford Escape was gone for the first time all week.

Good way to start the day!

With a cup of coffee in my hand, I trekked back up the stairs.

Back in my room, I sat the cup on the nightstand coaster, letting it cool a little while I made up the bed.

I need to change these sheets when I get off tomorrow.

When the bed was made up neatly and the throw pillows were perfectly placed, I sat down in my corner chair to enjoy my coffee.

"It's gonna be a good day," I manifested. "It's gonna be a good day where everybody goes home."

I grabbed my phone from the nightstand.

I had a missed call from my dad, three missed calls from Cassie, and none from Lena.

You need to figure out why this bothers you so much so you can get the fuck over it.

"I just think she deserves better than someone that doesn't value her," I talked to myself as I polished off my cup of coffee.

As I stood up to start the shower, my phone started to ring. I snatched it off the bed, excitedly, mildly disappointed to see that it was my dad.

I tapped the green square.

I faked enthusiasm. "Hey, Dad!"

"Hey, my buddy! How the hell are ya?"

I laughed. "I'm fine, Dad. How about you?"

"Doin' mighty fine. Heard the guys had a rough night last night. Were you workin'?"

This is on the list of shit I do not want to talk about right now.

"Yes, sir. Candle left burnin'."

"Sorry to hear it, buddy. I don't miss those days."

I forced myself to remain cheerful.

"All part of it, Dad."

"I know it."

Silence hung between us.

"I saw Lena yesterday." My ears perked up.

"Yeah?"

That didn't sound even remotely close to nonchalant.

"Yeah, she came by here. Told off Jace's mama in the lobby."

That was long overdue.

"I ain't even surprised. Linda has always been awful to her."

"I was proud of her - even if it did happen in the middle of the bank lobby."

I laughed.

"You know Lena. She will take the shit and take the shit, but when she hits her breakin' point - she blows a damn fuse."

"Oh, I know it. Speakin' of hotheaded…"

Here we go…

"How are things with Jace?"

"He is now on my shift startin' today."

Goddamnit. I had forgotten that until just now.

"Is that a good idea?" He sounded worried.

I sighed. "It will be fine. We both know the job comes first."

"What about Cassie? How are things there?"

Also on the list of shit I don't want to talk about right now.

"Dad, I'll come and talk to you about it all tomorrow when I come get Athens. I gotta get ready for work now."

"Aight, my buddy. I'll see you then. Stay safe out there. Love you!"

"Love you, Pops."

Despite ending the call with a smile, I jumped in the shower with fresh irritation, the mere mention of Jace killing my good mood.

Get there, do your job, and come the fuck home.

Jolene

I have new respect for my daddy.

I'd grown up on this farm, doing chores, but never to the degree that I'd done them today.

In Dad's defense, I did keep askin' for more work to do.

Every muscle in my body ached.

See, now I need the hot tub.

Snagging my phone from my jacket pocket, I checked my text messages. I was surprised to see that I had two texts from Cassie. She hadn't reached out since she sent that stupid picture message.

Meet you for five minutes to hear you out? To HEAR YOU OUT?

I locked my phone without responding, refusing to give the bitch one second of my time.

What could you possibly have to say that could be justified under the category of 'just hear me out'?

I twisted the knobs in my shower angrily. After stripping out of my work clothes, I pulled down my hair, combing my fingers through it as the bathroom filled with steam.

Hear her out…

I stepped into the shower, the water immediately attacking the tension in my neck. While I lathered my hair, I wrestled with the idea of what she could possibly have to say.

There was a part of me that didn't give a fuck about any explanation that came from her mouth but there was also a part of me that wanted to make her look me in the eye and explain how she could do this to me.

Other than just being a shitty person altogether.

I rinsed my hair quickly, careful to make sure I hadn't missed any of the dirt from the day. I used a rag to scrub my body, taking extra time on my most sensitive areas.

As I rubbed myself, I thought back to that night at the cabin when Dakota wrapped his lips around my clit.

The way he sucked it and flicked it with his tongue at the same time…

My pussy started tingling as I replayed it in my mind, my clit throbbing to be touched. I rolled it between my fingers, sending bits of pleasure splintering throughout my body. Sitting down on the seat inside of the shower, I teased and toyed, edging myself to the brink but never close enough to cum.

God, I want to feel him inside of me.

The way he stretched me just right and guided my hips as I rode him… The way he grunted my name when he came…The way he fucked my throat hard as if he wanted to hurt me, but with his hands cradling my head to make me feel safe…

I rubbed my clit faster, so fast my legs started to shake.

Dakota dipping his tongue inside me, making damn sure he got every single drop of cum… The way he begged me when I deepthroated him… the way he tasted on my tongue…

With every memory, I lost more of my control.

The way he fucked me from behind, the passion, the force…

With a moan, I exploded, my clit so sensitive that it ached.

Fuckkkkk.

With shaky legs, I attempted to stand.

The things I'd do to him right now would have me doused in holy water.

After bathing a second time, I stepped out of the shower. Feeling stronger and more determined as I wrapped the towel around me, I grabbed my phone from the vanity. Ignoring a text notification from Big Jake, I opened the text feed between me and Cassie.

Before I could change my mind, I told her to meet me in twenty minutes at Deja Brew.

Let me just go "hear her out" ...

Dakota

"Aight, y'all, I know last night was a tough one. Tonight will be better," I hyped them. "Let's get the ole girl inspected so we can all chill out until duty calls."

Zeke, Carter, Dedric, Ben, and Jace spread out to inspect the engine. While they checked off the truck, I inspected our air packs, cylinders, and PASS alarms to make sure everything was functioning properly.

Thirty minutes later, we were all inside the station, everybody busying themselves while waiting for the tones to drop. The station's phone rang and Jace answered it, his expression changing as he listened to the person on the other end of the line.

Lena would call his cell phone...wouldn't she?

After what seemed to be a fairly one-sided conversation, he hung the phone up on the wall. "DK?"

I walked over to the kitchen island. "What's up?"

"That was the PD. They wanted to let us know that they've arrested a few juveniles down by the Waverly Mill for trying to start fires. Apparently, it's part of some dumbass TikTok challenge. He recommended we stay on alert."

I nodded. "Whatever happened to talkin' someone's big brother into buyin' you a bottle of MD2020 and gettin' shitfaced in somebody's field? Teenagers these days are fuckin' stupid."

Jace nodded in agreement.

From the couch, Dedric piped up. "What's the Waverly Mill?"

"An old paper mill that closed down in the late nineties," I explained.

"And if that bitch ever catches fire, it will be a fuckin' worker," Jace added.

I gestured toward Jace. "What he said."

I wandered into my office. Opening my desk drawer, I pulled out my phone.

I only had one text message, and it was from Cassie; I deleted it without even looking at it.

Get it through your damn head.

Frustrated, I sat my phone on the desk.

"Don't know what to do with your hands, either, huh?" Jace spoke up from behind me.

What?

I spun my chair around to face him. "What do you mean?"

He leaned against the door frame. "Idle hands. I don't know what to do with them, either."

"Oh, I know what to do with my hands," I informed him. "I just can't do it right this minute."

He didn't respond and I knew I needed to bridge the gap.

"If you're bored, go shoot pool," I suggested. He stared down at his boots. "None of the guys like to play."

Oh yeah, I'm his pool buddy.

I forgot that I knew that.

He and I had gotten the pool table years ago, before one of the guys on B-Shift was medically retired, forcing Jace to transfer to cover him. He has been on that shift ever since so the only time we played was if one of us came up here off- duty.

"I'll let you get back to work, Lieutenant," he told me, leaving the office without waiting for a response.

Two hours down, the rest of my career to go.

Jolene

I sat outside of Deja Brew watching Cassie through the front window. She looked nervous, her hand coming up every so often to spin her earring.

Go see what she has to say, Lena.

Carefully avoiding the traffic on the main street, I hopped out of my car. The coffee shop's door alarm jingle-jangled as I pulled it open and stepped inside. Regretting my decision already, I walked over to the table where Cassie was waiting. Without a word, I sat down, the tension so thick, you could cut it with a knife. A smiling server made her way over to us.

"I see your friend made it! Would you like to order now?"

Friend...yeah, right.

I spoke up first, "I'll take a large cappuccino."

Cassie nodded. "I'll have what she's having." The server scurried off to make our drinks.

Not for the first time, apparently.

"Interesting choice of words," I pointed out dryly.

"What?"

"That you'll have what I'm havin'."

She turned beet red. "I…I didn't even think about it when I said it."

I sighed loudly. "What do you need to say, Cassie?"

Her eyes filled with tears. "I don't know where to begin," she admitted.

"Start with when you started sleepin' with my fiancé." The server appeared at the table the moment I finished the sentence, her mouth dropping open in shock. She sat our drinks down and hurried off without a word.

I stared at Cassie. "Well? When did it start?"

She hung her head. "Three years ago."

I know you fuckin' lyin'.

I felt the air seeping out of my lungs. "Who initiated it?"

She took a sip of her cappuccino. "I'm not sure, honestly. We were both drunk the first time."

When have you and Jace ever been drunk…wait a fuckin' minute.

"Drunk together… that means that Dakota and I were there."

She nodded.

I took a deep breath. "Why, Cassie?"

She folded her hands on the table. "The first time… like I said, we were drunk, so I don't know… but it continued because…because it wasn't supposed to. It was new. Dakota wasn't touching me, you weren't touching Jace. We used each other as an outlet for what we were missing."

I had to give it to her. The bitch had some balls to sit across from me, telling me all of this.

"Why the engagements and the wedding planning then?

"Because we love y'all."

Bullshit.

"Try again."

"I know it doesn't make sense, but we love y'all. I love you and Dak more than I can explain."

I felt a lump forming in the back of my throat.

Of all the shit she's divulged, is this what's going to make me cry?

"It's also because…" she trailed off.

"Because, what?" I prompted.

"Because we got off on making each other jealous."

So, my entire future was being planned because jealousy made the sex between the two of you hotter?

I felt like I was going to be sick.

"I'm going to sit here for sixty more seconds, Cassie. Say what you came here to say."

"I love Dakota, and I want to be with him. I don't want him feelin' like he has to choose between our relationship and your friendship. I think he already does so I would like for us to call a truce."

If this is the issue, we've got no issue.

"A truce? You want to call a truce over you fuckin' my fiancé inside the church, five minutes before my wedding was supposed to start?"

She hung her head.

"I want you to hear me clearly when I say this, Cass."

She looked me in the eyes.

"Fuck you," I told her.

With nothing else to say, I walked out of the café.

Dakota

Any man that tells you that the Top Gun scene where Goose dies – doesn't get to him a little bit –is either lying to you or has no soul.

The six of us were hanging out in the station's living room, watching the eighties classic and snacking on a vegetable tray.

"Wait, how did he die?" Dedric asked.

"His head hit the canopy when he ejected and it broke his neck," I explained.

"Nah, man, fuck this movie." He responded bitterly. "Y'all had me watchin' this whole damn movie for that shit!"

Everyone except him laughed.

"One of the best parts of this movie is — **riiiiiiing!**

We all leapt to our feet.

"Battalion 1, engine 11 – respond to 4447 Waverly Mills Road – 4447 Waverly Mills Road in reference to a structure fire.

Goddamnit!

We dressed out and loaded up – Jace, Dedric, and I in one truck, Ben, Carter and Zeke in another.

Jace, who was driving our engine, laid on the horn at folks that wouldn't pull over to make room for us to get through. "Move the fuck out the way!" he screamed.

Dedric grabbed ahold of the front seat, holding on as if his life depended on it.

"Easy, Jace," I muttered. "Get us there alive, bud."

"This is gonna be a bitch!" Jace yelled looking over at me. I nodded; my eyes fixed on the road ahead.

The air grew hazy as we neared the old papermill.

"Aight, Rook, this will be your biggest one yet so keep your eyes open and remember what you know!" I hollered over the siren.

He nodded; his eyes glazed over in fear.

We pulled up to the mill, the flames already blowing out of the side.

"Goddamn…"

We piled out in unison with the rest of our guys. "Zeke, hydrant, Rook, nozzle, the rest of you, primary. Everybody is goin' home, repeat it!"

"Everybody is goin' home!"

A group of teenagers were gathered near the entrance to the building, hollering and acting a fool. "Anybody inside?!"

One of the girls turned to us, screaming, "There's five of our friends in there! Go get them!"

Grabbing my mic, I locked eyes with Jace.

"Battalion 1, engine 11 – on scene – working structure fire – five possible entrapment – establishing primary search – 1211 requesting mutual aid."

"Command – 1211 – toning mutual aid."

Jace, Carter, Ben and I began our primary search.

Carter got the first rescue, a teenage girl around the age of fifteen. I grabbed the second, a seventeen-year-old boy. Jace was right behind me with a third, a fourteen-year-old boy.

With two unaccounted for, we went back in just as mutual aid showed up on scene.

I was midway through the warehouse when the ceiling started to creak, a sure sign it was time to pull out of the search.

"1211 to Command – be advised – primary search is being terminated. Any active search & rescue evacuate immediately – primary search terminated."

I crawled towards the exit; there was about sixty yards before I was out. I watched as Jace or maybe, it was Carter, exited the building, a small bit of relief flooding my veins. The ceiling panels were falling all around me, igniting flames where there originally were none. A flaming portion of the wall collapsed in front of me, the door no longer in sight. I scanned my surroundings for a way around the blaze, but there didn't seem to be one for me to find. The fire was spreading quickly, engulfing another wall nearby.

"Command – 1211 – requesting status of S&R"

I crawled over the smoldering debris, doing my best to stay low with my head down.

"1211 to Command. I'm tryin'!"

An interior wall fell against me, knocking my oxygen tank loose on my back.

"Battalion Chief to S&R – get the fuck out!"

I'm tryin', Chief.

Using my axe, I cleared a path, suddenly able to see the flicker of emergency light. The fire rippled above my head, but I still felt nothing but exhaustion and relief.

Almost there, Dak.

My oxygen mask felt like it was starting to malfunction, the air getting harder and harder to breathe. I forced myself to crawl a few more feet, but then, I just couldn't go anymore. I closed my eyes for what felt like, years.

"Chief! DK! Right here!" I felt someone grab the top of my coat. All at once, I felt stronger than ever, that strength fueled by the determination of my team. The flashing lights were the first thing I saw as Carter and Zeke guided me over to the truck.

Fuck, that was close.

I removed my useless air mask and did a once over of all of my guys.

Zeke, Carter, Ben, Dedric... where's Jace?

"Chief! Where's Jace?!"

He and I locked eyes as he realized what I'd asked him.

I snatched the radio off the tailboard of the truck.

"Mayday! Mayday! Mayday! We have a firefighter down!"

Throwing down the radio, I took off towards the warehouse.

"Clayton, get back here!" Chief Hennessy hollered. "Dakota!!"

Dropping to my knees, I crawled back inside the inferno, screaming out for my oldest friend in the world.

My lungs burned without my mask on, the pain making it harder to breathe. I crawled across the warehouse, doing my best to keep my distance from the waves of fire that were dancing over my head.

I screamed his name as hard as my chest would allow.

After shoving a table out of the way, I paused to listen out for his PASS alarm.

It's not beeping so he's moving.

Ignoring the pain, I kept on crawling, the panic starting to set in. A crash behind me confirmed the worst of my fears – the ceiling at the entrance had collapsed. With a terror in my voice that even I didn't recognize, I screamed at the top of my lungs. "Jace!! We gotta get outta here!" As I inched my way, propped up on my elbows, I heard a beeping sound from somewhere nearby. The fire was behind me, but it was walking my way and taking away precious time with every inch that it spread.

"Jace! Stay with me, brother, I'm comin'!!"

I've got to find him. Not just for him and for me, but for Lena. That's the love of her life.

His alarm grew louder, both a blessing and a curse, until I finally caught the reflectives on his coat with my flashlight.

Thank you, Lord.

"Jace! C'mon brother, we're goin'!" I snatched him to his feet were he collapsed against me. Through his mask, I could see his eyes were closed. "Wake up, Jace. Everybody goin' home, remember! We goin' home!"

I dragged both of us towards what, I prayed, was a window since everything behind us was on fire.

Please, God, let it be a window.

Relief overtook me as I saw that it was, knowing we would make it out of the building.

"Almost there, buddy, stay with me!" I gasped, my lungs damn near close to giving up. "Tell me what you got me for Christmas!"

The fire was starting to roll over us, the sound of portions of the ceiling coming down all around us. With my elbow, I knocked the glass out of the frame. With what felt like the last bit of strength that I had left, I shoved him out the window.

He landed with a thud about four feet down. My lungs decided it was the end of the line as I went out the window behind him.

With what seemed like the last breath in my body, I used his mic to call out. **"We out."**

Lying next to my buddy, I closed my eyes and gave in to the sweet darkness.

Jolene

"Welcome to The Southern Sizzler! My name is Anna. How y'all folks doin' tonight?"

"Well, Miss Anna," my daddy spoke up, "I get the pleasure of takin' my two favorite girls out to supper tonight, so I couldn't be better. How are you?"

I've said it before and I'll say it again, the world does not deserve my daddy.

"I'm wonderful!" Anna beamed. "Thank you for askin'! Can I get y'all somethin' to drink?"

We all ordered a Miller Lite. "Be back in a jiff," Anna promised.

Mama turned to me. "How was your day, sugar? What did you do?"

"I worked with daddy on the farm for most of the day," I started, "then, I met up with Cassie in the afternoon."

They both stopped buttering their roll.

"How did that go?" Dad asked, giving me his undivided attention. I shrugged in what I was hoped was a nonchalant fashion. "She told me how long the affair had been goin' on, and she asked for a truce for Dak's sake."

Mama rolled her eyes, but daddy's interest was piqued. "How long did it go on?"

I sighed. "Three years."

Daddy dropped his knife. Mama's mouth hung open in disbelief.

Same, y'all, same.

Anna approached the table with a tray that held our drinks.

"Anna," Dad began, "Shug, I'm gonna need a Jack on the rocks."

From somewhere inside my purse, my phone started to ring.

Nope, not today, Satan.

I ignored it until it stopped.

"So, what else did you find out, Lee Lee?" Mama asked me.

Where do I even begin?

"So, she said the first –," I was interrupted by my phone ringing once again.

"See who it is. Might be important," Daddy told me. I fumbled in my purse until I found my phone.

Two missed calls from the fire chief?

"Who was it, honey?" Mama asked me.

"Chief Hennessy," I told her, puzzled at why he would be calling me.

"Call him back."

Before I could dial his number, he was calling me again.

"Lena, you need to come to the hospital. There was a warehouse fire. He's…he's in bad shape, Lee Lee."

My heart dipped down into my stomach.

A warehouse fire…

"Okay, I'm comin' right now."

"See you soon."

I hung up my phone.

"What's the matter, sweetie?" Mama asked.

"Dakota…," I choked out. "Warehouse fire. Chief said he's in bad shape. I gotta go."

I ran out of the restaurant without waiting for their response.

The chief's words played on a loop in my head as I frantically drove towards the hospital.

"He's in bad shape, Lee Lee."

Traffic was light for this time of night, making it a quick, easy trip.

Why didn't I talk to him this mornin' when he needed a friend? Why wasn't I there for him the way he's been there for me?

The hospital parking lot was full of emergency vehicles, more than I'd ever seen in one place.

Oh my God.

After peeling into the nearest available space, I jumped out of my car without even bothering to grab my keys.

I sprinted across the parking lot, bypassing a cluster of deputies near the front door. After making it through the rotating door, I stormed the check-in desk in the lobby.

"Hi, my name is Jolene Felder and I'm lookin' for –"

"Lee Lee," Chief Hennessy interrupted.

I whirled around.

"Chief, where is he?" I cried out, my voice quaking with the promise of tears. He put his arm around me. "I'll take you, honey."

He led me down a hallway to a door labeled Trauma 3.

"Go on in, punkin. I'm right behind you."

With trembling hands, I twisted open the doorknob.

There he lay in a tiny emergency room bed, an oxygen tube situated firmly against his nose. His cheek was cut open with a fresh pair of stitches, and almost every inch of his visible skin was covered with soot. He looked fragile and terrible, like you'd break him with one touch, but the most noticeable thing about him was that he wasn't Dakota, at all.

Jace…

"Wait, it's Jace?"

Chief Hennessy looked as if he didn't understand the question. "Yes, that's Jace…," he explained gently.

I can see who it is… where the fuck is, Dakota?

"Dak…," I asked him. "Where is Dak?"

Realization brimmed in his eyes as he understood what I'd been thinking.

"He's on a different floor. I'll take you."

Leaving Jace's room, we passed by the nurses' station where a gaggle of deputies were standing by.

"What happened, Chief?" I asked hesitantly, unsure if I wanted to know.

Pressing the button on the old elevator, he turned to me with tears in his eyes. "A bunch of damn kids started a fire at the old papermill. DK – Dak, to you, and Jace were on search and rescue. Dakota had to be helped out of the warehouse but when we saw that Jace was missing, he called mayday and went back in after him."

Holy fuck.

As we stepped off the elevator, he volunteered more as we walked down the old corridor.

"I screamed to Dak to keep him from goin' back in. He didn't have his oxygen or mask. I hollered until I couldn't see him anymore, but you know how that boy is…" he trailed off.

"Everybody is goin' home," I quoted Dak's mantra.

The chief nodded with tears in his eyes.

"This is Dak's room."

The sign on his door said ICU 8 – Clayton.

Intensive care…

A nurse came rushing down the hall. "Chief Hennessy, we are monitoring him closely so please make sure we limit visitation to immediate family and the guys from the station," she looked pointedly at me.

Bitch, I will rip this door off the goddamn hinges.

The chief felt me tense up beneath his arm and understood that I was about to choose violence.

"Lena is family," he explained calmly. "We won't visit him long."

He pulled open the heavy door and held it there, allowing me to walk in the room first.

Dakota was lying there shirtless, with a brace on his left arm. He had stitches and gauze, just above his left eye, and some bandages covering a part of his neck. His tattooed chest seemed to be the least damaged of all, pumping up and down as it should, but as I noticed the hose that was attached to his mouth, I realized it wasn't pumping up and down on its own.

"He's on a ventilator." Chief Hennessy explained. "It's takin' over breathing for him for a bit so he can rest. They've also mentioned doing a medically induced coma due to the degree of smoke inhalation and burns inside of his lungs."

As I stared in disbelief, a lump formed in the back of my throat.

"I'll give y'all a minute, Lee Lee, but remember, he needs to rest."

I nodded tearfully. "Thanks, Chief."

"He obviously can't speak but he might be able to hear you so give him a good ass chewin' for me, will ya?" he asked right before leaving the room.

I walked a little closer to his bedside, hating how small he looked in the giant ass bed.

"Okay, you've made your point. You're great at your job," I teased him softly as I picked up his large, dirty hand.

The tube down his throat looked more hazardous than helpful. "I feel like this would be the perfect time to use that thing you say about how you look cuter with something in your mouth so I'm goin' to need you to wake up so I can say it to you."

The ventilator whooshed, the quiet sound screaming at me louder than anything I'd ever heard.

Squeezing his hand, I started to cry. "I changed my mind about the hot tub… but you can't get in there with all this shit on so you gotta get better, okay?"

I silently begged for him to open his eyes, for him to give me any sign that he was actually alive.

"Chief said you saved some kids and then ran back in after Jace… if I've never told you before…"

And in case I never get the chance to again.

"I'm proud of you. I'm proud to call you my friend."

There was a gentle knock at the door and a middle-aged man stuck his head inside. "Hi, I'm Dr Bowers," he stepped inside. "Are you his spouse?"

"No," I sighed. "But I can call her."

After promising Dakota I'd be back with some whiskey, I kissed his head before leaving the room.

Chief Hennessy was waiting for me down the hall.

"The doctor asked me if I was his wife," I informed him. "I told him I would call her."

Neither of us said a word as we rode the elevator downstairs because neither of us knew what to say.

We were back on the first floor, easing our way towards the trauma unit, when he finally figured out what to say. "I make it my business to mind my own business… but are you sure he would want you to call Cassie?

I mean, yes, but also maybe, no?

"I don't know," I admitted. He nodded. "I called Jake. He's on the way."

"Okay."

We rounded the nurse's station.

"Listen, Lena, I know it's not the best timing, but you are Jace's power of attorney. The doctor would like to speak with you."

"I don't want to be his power of attorney," I spoke firmly.

"I know, but I think he has to change it. I can't change it for him," he sympathized.

That man has been cheatin' on me for three years. If y'all let me make decisions for him, I'm gonna wind up doin' that man like Helen did Charles.

"Okay."

He escorted me back to Jace's hospital room where a young woman wearing a white coat, was waiting near the door.

"Hi, Mrs. Reynolds, I'm Dr. Jurgens," she explained, extending her hand.

Not Mrs. Reynolds.

"Hi," I responded, shaking her hand, "my name is Jolene Felder."

"My apologies. Ok, so just a quick update on Jace," she began. "He didn't sustain much damage from smoke inhalation since he kept his mask on, but he does have a few broken ribs, lacerations, and a fractured collarbone. We will likely keep him for observation for the next two days to run a few more tests, but I'm confident he will make a full recovery"

Next to me, Chief Hennessy breathed a sigh of relief.

"I appreciate it, Dr. Jurgens," I thanked her. She smiled warmly. "He's awake in there now, asking for you."

"I'll go check on him," I assured her.

With a nod, she headed off towards the nurse's station.

The fire chief spoke up, "You go on in, Lena. I'll go wait on Jake."

His eyes look so tired.

I nodded.

As I turned the door handle, I had an epiphany.

"Hey, Chief?" I called out to him. He turned around.

"Is the rest of the team okay?"

He clasped his hands together in front of his chest. "Yes, thank the Lord."

Hallelujah.

I held my breath as I entered Jace's room.

"Hey, Lenie," he managed.

"You look like shit."

Be nice, Lena.

He laughed at my words, wincing at the pain in his ribs.

"You should see the other guy," he joked.

Stop tryin' to be normal.

I pulled a chair up to the side of his bed.

"You need to change your power of attorney to your mama."

His face fell. "I trust your decision-making skills more than I trust hers."

That's a mistake.

"You don't need to trust my decision makin'," I told him flatly. "If there was a machine keepin' you alive right now, I just might unplug it to charge my phone."

"I wouldn't blame you."

"Three years, Jace. You looked at me every day for three years and lied to me."

He stared down at his hands. "You'll never know how much I regret it." He looked up with tears running down his cheeks.

"I didn't deserve that. Neither did Dak."

His eyes lit up as he remembered why he was here. "Where is Dakota?"

"In ICU on a vent."

He broke down in tears. "He's in there because of me. He pulled me out of the building."

I nodded. "He's good at his job."

"Most people would have just left me there. That's what I would have wanted to do if the situation were reversed."

I stood up from the uncomfortable hospital chair.

"I guess you are lucky that Dakota is a better man than you," I poured salt in his wounds. "Feel better soon."

Without another word, I turned and left his room.

Dakota

Two Weeks Later

My throat is on fuckin' fire.

I opened my eyes.

Where the fuck am I?

"Dakota!" my dad's voice rang out. "You're awake!"

He appeared at my bedside, looking like he had slept under a bridge.

"You look like hell, Pops."

"Well, your youngin' bein' in a coma for over two damn weeks will mess with one's quality of life!"

Two weeks?

"Why am I here?" I croaked.

He looked alarmed. "You don't remember the Waverly Mills fire?"

I didn't respond to him, but it all came flooding back to me.

Lena, Cassie, the fire, those teenagers, Mayday, lost air pack, Jace…

"Jace! Is Jace alright?!"

My dad nodded proudly. "You saved his life," he beamed. "I'm gonna go get Dr. Bowers."

He quickly left the room.

Jace is alright. We got out.

The door burst open, and a doctor walked in.

"Hey, Lt. Clayton, I'm Dr. Bowers. How are you feelin'?"

"Like I got my ass kicked," I admitted. "Where is Lena?"

"Lena…the brunette? That's your fiancé, correct?"

"Lena is blonde, and I do not have a fiancé."

"My mistake, I was under the impression that –"

"I understand," I interrupted. "But I don't want that brunette anywhere near me. Can I add that to some sort of list somehow?"

"Certainly. I'll have your nurse come in and take care of that, but first, can you follow this light for me, using just your eyes?"

I followed the light.

"Excellent! Can you lift your right arm and your left leg simultaneously?"

I did as he asked.

After a series of other tests, he seemed confident that I was thinking clearly and on the right track.

Where the hell did my dad go?

"How's your pain on a scale of 1-10?" Dr. Bowers asked.

I thought it over. "Maybe a three."

"Wonderful! Okay, I'm going to send your nurse in to handle your situation with your visitor list and I'll be back to check in on you later."

"Thanks, Doc."

I tried to sit up, but my ass felt like it was numb.

Where the hell did my dad go!?

Where the hell is my phone and where the hell is Lena?

I fumbled around for the bed's remote, but the bitch was nowhere to be found. Frustrated, I gave up and closed my eyes.

"Happy New Year, shithead," a sweet voice rang out.

My eyes flew open. "Loo!"

She looked like she wanted to cry as she came into the room, and I held out my arm for a hug. "Come here, pal."

She walked over to the bed, her bottom lip trembling more with every step that she took. She was doing her best to keep a straight face, but I'd known her for far too long.

She gave me a quick hug as if she thought she might hurt me, the smell of her shampoo smacking me right in the face.

She stared at the IV that was in the crease of my arm, her brow furrowed with thoughts she wouldn't say.

 I reached out for her hand. "I'm okay, Lena Loo."

"I know you love a good nap, but sixteen days is just excessive," she teased. "It's literally a different year!"

I laughed, the pain reverberating across my spine. "You know I'm an over-achiever." Her lip quivered and all I wanted to do was kiss it away.

"How are ya, Loo?"

"I'm okay."

"How's Jace?"

"Good, I guess."

You guess?

"You don't know?"

"Not really," she admitted. "I haven't seen him since he was discharged from the hospital."

Oh, shit.

"Have you been to visit me?"

"Every day," my dad informed me from the doorway. "She comes before work, on her lunch break, and after work."

I looked at Lena. "Is that true?"

She nodded.

Joining her at the bedside, he put his arm around her.

"Ask her what she did on Christmas Eve," he prompted.

I looked up at her. "What did you do?" I asked curiously.

She rolled her eyes. "I slept in the rocker so Santa could find you. I knew I was on the nice list, and you weren't, so I did you a solid." She pointed across the room. "Once he got here, he felt bad that you looked like that, so he left you some stuff anyways."

Dad pressed the button on the arm rail, adjusting my bed, so I could see what she was pointing at.

Oh, my goodness...

On a small table in the corner of the room was a small Christmas tree with a few wrapped gifts underneath it, alongside an overly filled stocking.

"Damn, it looks like I did make the nice list."

"Only by association," Lena pointed out. "I told you – that's why I stayed."

I rolled my eyes at her, but I felt like I was bursting as the seams.

I'm in love with her.

That realization was the only clear thought in my mind.

My dad interrupted my thoughts with some thoughts of his own.

"I guess I should call Cassie and tell her that you're awake."

I held up my hand. "Don't bother. I'm waitin' on a nurse to come in so I can officially add her to the visitation ban list," I informed him. "She told Dr. Bowers that she was my fiancé."

Lena looked at me guiltily. "I told him that she was your fiancé."

What the fuck?

"What? Why?"

"Because I thought she was? She was still livin' with you when you got hurt!" She defended herself.

"Because she refused to fuckin' leave!" I shouted.

I was starting to get a headache.

"Ok, simmer down before you short circuit a brain cell," my dad joked. "Lena was doin' what she thought was best and she has tried very hard to get along with Cassie, for your sake."

"I have!" Lena chimed in. "So, you're welcome, Jackass."

Maybe I'm not bein' clear.

"Cassie isn't my anything. I don't want you to be nice to her, for me, and I don't want to be anywhere near her."

Failing to hide her smile, Lena nodded.

Can I just tell her I love her?

"I love you, Lena."

Okay, you didn't even give all your brain cells time to decide!

She rolled her eyes. "Love you, too. Most of the time."

She's not gettin' it.

"No, I need you to listen."

She smiled. "I am listening. The whole floor is listening. Why are you hollerin'?"

Because you are not fuckin' listening.

"Dad, can you give us a minute?"

"Sure thing, I'll go call Brett and let them know you're awake!"

He left my room.

I looked at Lena. "Climb in here with me," I ordered. She looked at me like I had lost my mind. "In your bed?"

"Yes."

"Dak, no. You are healing and I don' –"

"Lena, please."

She sighed in frustration, but she climbed up on the edge of the bed.

"I'm worried I'm goin' to snag a wire," she confessed.

Fuck these wires.

"I think I'm in love with you."

She looked like she had seen a ghost.

That's not the reaction you want when you tell someone that.

"Why do you think that?" She asked quietly.

"Before this happened, you were the first thought in my head when I woke up, the person I wanted to talk to all day, the person I wanted to make a bad day better, the last thought in my head before I fell asleep," I rambled. "The day of the fire, when I woke up that mornin', and I saw you hadn't texted or called me, I thought it was because you were back with Jace. He had told me the day before that you had been at his house…"

She waited silently for me to continue.

"When I ran back in there after him, I was determined to find him because I didn't want you to feel the pain of losin' him. I'd have gone back in for him either way – that's my brother – but the thought of the chief having to tell you he didn't make it… it kept me going. When I realized that all of it, no matter the risk, was worth it so long as you didn't feel pain… I knew I loved you."

I watched as tears fell in her lap.

Now I'm the one causing her pain.

I tilted her chin up to look her in the eye. "Tell me what you're thinkin', Lena."

"I'm scared."

Me, too.

"So am I," I admitted." But I know that this is different."

"How?"

"Because I'm goin' to love you either way."

She looked confused.

"What do you mean?"

"If you choose to walk out of here right now and never speak to me again, I'm still goin' to choose to love you. Even if it's not the same for you – even if you aren't in love with me – I'll still choose this every day because just being able to love you is enough for me."

That was a shit ton of information for her in ninety seconds.

She opened her mouth to speak but a knock at the door interrupted her.

"Come in," I invited.

The door crept open and in walked Cassie, her face lighting up when she saw that I was awake.

"Ooh, I lied. Don't come in. Go back out."

Lena swatted at me. "Stop. She loves you, too, and she's been worried to death."

Too? Does that mean you love me?

Cassie stepped up to the foot of my bed.

"I just wanted to make sure that you are okay," she told me, an obvious sadness weighing down her voice.

Lena tried to pull her hand out of mine, but I did nothing but tighten my grasp.

"I'm fine, Cass. In fact, I'm better than I've been in a long time. I was just tellin' Lena that I'm in love with her."

It was a toss-up of whose eyes grew wider – the woman I wanted or the one I'd never want again.

"How can that even be possible? We just broke up," Cassie pointed out tearfully.

You were literally with someone while we were still together…

"I'll let you two talk," Lena spoke up, effectively snatching her hand away from mine.

"I don't want to talk anymore, Lena. I just want you to curl up in this bed with me and take a nap."

She looked at me like I was being ridiculous while Cassie sobbed at the foot of the bed.

Through her tears, she spoke bitterly, "So, that's it? You're throwing away everything that we built together?"

Happily.

"Yes. I'm starting this new thing where I throw away things that are trash."

She stared at me for a few seconds before leaving the room, quietly shutting the door behind her.

The moment the door closed, Lena jumped up from the bed. Radiating anger, she put her hands on her hips.

"Why the hell would you do that?! She's a shitty person but she was worried and that's the first thing you say to her?!"

Grabbing ahold of her shirt, I yanked her into my arms.

"I told you… when you're in love with someone, you don't want to hide it."

Epilogue

Jolene

"Mama, we're gonna be late!" I called out impatiently from the entryway.

"I'm comin', Lee Lee!"

Slow as molasses.

She emerged from her bedroom with my daddy right behind her.

"Daddy, you're comin', too?"

"Yes. Dakota is bein' named Firefighter of the Year. Of course, I'm comin'!"

Smiling, I opened the front door, the spring breeze sending my hair flying.

"Big Jake is waiting for us so let's go!"

Loading up in my daddy's truck, we set off towards the civic center. Unsurprisingly, the parking lot was packed, the people of Creek's Edge coming out in droves.

"All of these people are here to support your man," Mama teased. Laughing, I climbed out of my dad's truck.

Big Jake met us just inside the entrance, an enormous grin on his face.

"Hey, daughter!" he greeted me with a hug. "How's my favorite girl doin'?"

Even though Dakota and I had only been dating a few months, he had taken up calling me his daughter. He was as overjoyed as my parents about the new relationship, and it was crazy because not much had actually changed. It's just being with my long-time best friend all the time but with some incredibly hot sex thrown in the game.

The things that man can do with his tongue…

"Let's find our seats!" Mama piped up excitedly.

As we walked down the aisle towards the section labeled reserved, I spotted Cassie with her new boyfriend, a deputy from Creek's Edge Sheriff's Office. She smiled at me, and I waved at them both, happy to see that she was happy.

Things between her and I would never be the same, but I had hope for the future going forward.

As Chief Hennessy took to the stage, a silence fell over the crowd.

"Good evening, ladies and gentlemen and welcome! Tonight, we will recognize some local heroes that represent excellence, bravery, and brotherhood. Heroes that are the very definition of 'the first in, the last out'. With that, I would like to ask Carter Neyland and Jace Reynolds to join me on stage."

Carter and Jace, dressed sharply in their Class A uniform, joined the chief on stage where he placed a medal around their neck and presented them each with a plaque.

"It is my pleasure to present the both of you with the Firefighter Excellence Achievement award. The both of you have proven your dedication and determination, not only to this team, but most importantly, the community."

Applause broke out amongst the crowd, our row clapping hardest of all.

They deserve this so much.

On the stage, Jace stepped up to the microphone.

"I speak for myself and for Carter when I say thank you to our community for this incredible honor. Being a firefighter is one of those jobs where you have to do it in order to understand how quickly things can go from calm to chaos," he spoke eloquently. "You have to do it to understand how important it is to have this camaraderie with the guys that you work with. Last December, we had a night that changed the way we worked as a team, the way we viewed the world, and especially, the way we viewed each other. I can tell you with absolute certainty that I am only standing here today because of the heart and the courage of someone else on our team. A man that exemplifies professionalism, dedication, and loyalty, even to those that – trust me – do not deserve it," his voice wavered. "I'm able to stand before you today because of his selflessness and bravery. With that, I'd like to introduce you to our Firefighter of the Year, Lieutenant Dakota Clayton."

Thunderous applause erupted throughout the auditorium. People began to stand up, our row joining in the ovation with tears in our eyes.

Dak walked up on stage proudly, hugging Chief Hennessy and Carter on his way over to the podium.

Jace placed a large medal over his head and presented him with his award, a moment of eye contact being shared between the two. They hugged like the best friends they no longer were, mutual respect, gratefulness, and memories taking them over.

With tears streaming down my cheeks, I stole a glance at Cassie. She happened to be staring right back at me, her eyes filled with tears to match mine. I smiled at her, and she smiled back, an unspoken agreement of how proud of them we were.

Dakota took over the podium with a huge smile on his face.

"I'd like to thank the folks of Creek's Edge for this honor. Being named Firefighter of the Year just seems like the Lord is playin' favorites considering I get to do something I love, and I get to do it with family," he gestured towards his team. "I couldn't do this job without my brothers at Engine Company 11, my family, and one pretty special girl."

Ooh, he's gettin' his soul sucked out tonight.

"If I could," he continued. "I'd like to ask her to come up on stage."

I'm gonna beat his ass.

After squeezing my way past everyone on our row, I nervously walked up on stage.

As he stood at the podium, he reached for my hand, his eyes brighter than I'd ever seen them before.

"Lena, Lord knows, I never expected to be here. You've been my irritating best friend for nearly two decades and I was happy with the way that worked out… but then something changed, and I started wanting to plan out forever, and that was terrifying for me because I never even planned on loving you… but now that it's happened, I know I can't go back to anything that's less than loving all of you, every single day. And the only conclusion I've came to – to make sure that happens – is that you've gotta let me marry you."

The auditorium went unbelievably insane as he dropped to one knee, pulling a ring box out of his pocket.

Tearfully, I nodded, with an absolute "yes."

As he pulled me into his arms, I pressed my lips to his ear. "Why did you make your day all about us?!"

He pulled away, grinning, with a gleam in his eye.

"I told you, Lena Loo. When you love someone, you don't want to hide it."

343